DEAD ON CUE

Recent Titles by Deryn Lake from Severn House

The Reverend Nick Lawrence Mysteries

THE MILLS OF GOD
DEAD ON CUE

The Apothecary John Rawlings Mysteries

DEATH AND THE BLACK PYRAMID
DEATH AT THE WEDDING FEAST

DEAD ON CUE

A Reverend Nick Lawrence Mystery

Deryn Lake

This first world edition published 2012
in Great Britain and 2013 in the USA by
SEVERN HOUSE PUBLISHERS LTD of
19 Cedar Road, Sutton, Surrey, England, SM2 5DA.
Trade paperback edition first published
in Great Britain and the USA 2013 by
SEVERN HOUSE PUBLISHERS LTD .

British Library Cataloguing in Publication Data

Lake, Deryn.
  Dead on cue.
  1. Police--England--Sussex--Fiction. 2. Vicars,
  Parochial--England--Sussex--Fiction. 3. Murder--
  Investigation--England--Sussex--Fiction. 4. Detective
  and mystery stories.
  I. Title
  823.9'2-dc23

ISBN-13: 978-0-7278-8226-4 (cased)
ISBN-13: 978-1-84751-460-8 (trade paper)

All Severn House titles are printed on acid-free paper.

Severn House Publishers support The Forest Stewardship Council [FSC],
the leading international forest certification organisation. All our titles that
are printed on Greenpeace-approved FSC-certified paper carry the FSC logo.

MIX
Paper from
responsible sources
FSC
www.fsc.org   FSC® C018575

Typeset by Palimpsest Book Production Ltd.,
Falkirk, Stirlingshire, Scotland.
Printed and bound in Great Britain by
MPG Books Ltd., Bodmin, Cornwall.

In memory of my little half-sister, Petrea Elizabeth, who died when she was four hours old.
How different things might have been.

ACKNOWLEDGEMENTS

My most profound thanks to my friend and colleague Jean McConnell, who wrote and directed the Son et Lumière at Tonbridge Castle on which my story is based. Both myself and my two children were fortunate enough to act in this wonderful show and I can truly say that it was one of the great experiences of all our lives. I have never been better directed and how one small woman could amass and control that enormous cast is a stupendous feat. Bravo Jean. And may your play, *Deckchairs*, for which you are better known, be acted for evermore.

ONE

The smell of an early autumn bonfire drifted by his nostrils as Nick Lawrence dozed in a striped deckchair on a Saturday afternoon. It was a pleasant aroma, vaguely reminiscent of marmalade and marijuana. He had eaten the first but never smoked the latter, though he had once sniffed the air at a party and been informed by a giggling girl that that was what the unknown fragrance had been, adding to his somewhat limited knowledge of the subject. Beside him, on a small garden table, stood a portable radio from which the low and somehow comforting voice of a cricket commentator was speaking in a steady monotone. On his lap, perched rather uncomfortably, sat Radetsky, a mass of purring ginger fur. It was a golden early autumn day, it was a Saturday, and the Reverend Nicholas Lawrence was taking his ease. And then inside the vicarage the telephone began to ring. Coming back to full consciousness, Nick uttered a mild curse, removed Radetsky from his resting place, and made his way indoors.

The voice at the other end was extremely flustered. 'Oh, Father Nick, I do hope I haven't disturbed you.'

'No, not at all, Mavis. I was in the garden, that's all. What can I do for you?'

'Well, I've just shown a most interesting man round the church and he says he is extremely anxious to meet you. To cut a long story short –' as if his churchwarden possibly could, Nick thought – 'he has just moved into the village – only been here a week – and says he wants to take part in every aspect of village life. There's only one snag that I can see – and that would apply to the older folk, of course, not the younger set.' Mavis laughed gaily.

'And that is?'

'He's black.'

'Really, Mavis,' said the vicar severely, 'you shouldn't say such things. A man is a man, regardless of the colour of his skin.'

'Oh, I know that, Father Nick, indeed I do. I was just thinking of poor old Mrs Deakin.'

'Well, she will just have to get on with it. Racial prejudice is a thing of the past and the sooner she gets that through her head the better.'

'But she's ninety-four,' Mavis protested.

Nick smiled sadly. There were some things to which there was absolutely no answer. He changed the subject.

'What's the name of the newcomer?'

'Gerry Harlington. He gave me a card. I think he's an American. He had quite a strong accent.'

'Is he attending church tomorrow?'

'Says he wouldn't miss it for the world.'

'Good. I shall make a point of speaking to him.'

'Oh please do, Father. I know he'll appreciate it.'

'I shall be certain to make him welcome. Now, is there anything else I can help you with?'

'No, Vicar.'

'Good, then I'll see you in church.'

Nick put down the phone and walked back into the garden. Radetsky had taken his place in the deckchair. Nick shoved him off and resumed his earlier position, turning the radio up a little louder. But this time he remained wide awake, thinking about the extraordinary village of Lakehurst and its strange mixture of inhabitants, many of whom seemed caught in a time warp.

He had come to the parish, newly appointed by Bishop Claude, exactly a year ago, Nick thought to himself as Radetsky whizzed on to his lap once more. And what a time that had been. Almost within days of his arrival a serial killer had struck, killing at random, a diseased and cruel mind apparently, yet all along there had been one intended victim. And by a fluke Nick had actually been able to help the police with the clue that linked the whole ghastly affair into one neat pattern.

Nick smiled to himself as Radetsky turned three times then settled down. The police had been represented on that occasion by Inspector Dominic Tennant, he of the gooseberry-green eyes and pixieish charm. The vicar had the feeling that Tennant must have been quite an innovation in the Sussex force bringing about, no doubt, mixed emotions from his fellow officers. His assistant,

Detective Sergeant Potter, had been far more what one imagined a policeman would be like. Young, straightforward, somewhat unimaginative, but fiercely loyal to his superior officer. Nick had liked them both and wished that it had been possible to have kept in more regular contact.

The cricket commentary ended and Nick glanced at his watch. It was six o'clock and time for the evening news. He removed the cat and went into the house to switch the television on. An hour later found him in The Great House downing a pint before going home to cook his supper and have a reasonably early night. It had been a joyfully quiet Saturday with no weddings, no services, no parish duties, nothing but a long glorious day to himself. Yet, despite the presence of the cat and William − Nick's noisy but cheerful resident ghost − he had experienced the occasional pang of solitude and with them had come thoughts of Olivia Beauchamp.

She had not been around in Lakehurst for quite some while, booked for a world tour that would last for months. Nick had received a postcard from China and had imagined her, dark head bent over the violin, her enigmatic beauty smouldering, playing to a strangely quiet audience until the end when they would burst into loud and sustained applause. He could almost see her taking her bow, slim as a reed in her sulky red dress, her black hair tossing back as the conductor kissed her hand.

His reverie was spoilt by a voice saying politely, 'Good evening, Nick.'

He looked up from his pint to see that Dr Kasper Rudniski had joined him. Tonight the doctor looked dreamy in a pair of jeans made of dark-blue denim that fitted like a second skin. Above these he had a crisp white shirt with ballooning sleeves that made him resemble a Russian doll. It had clearly been purchased in Poland and was of a style that Nick remembered in the sixties. However, everything looked good on the handsome doctor and there was the usual small murmur from the barmaids and various other young females as he walked into the bar.

'Hello, Kasper,' answered Nick, and wondered if the doctor and Olivia had ever exchanged a passionate kiss. But such thoughts were banished by the sudden sound of Jack Boggis, sitting in his usual place − back turned, facing the wall − chortling loudly at a piece in the *Daily Telegraph*.

Kasper looked at Nick, raised an eyebrow and said, '*Plus ça change.*'

It seemed to the vicar that ever since time began Jack Boggis had been sitting in the same chair in the same pub reading the same paper and would continue to do so until at last his corpse was discovered in the same position, stiff as a board, still holding a pint to its purplish lips. He grinned to himself and muttered his thoughts into Kasper's ear. And there they were, giggling like a couple of schoolboys, when the outer door opened and footsteps could be heard approaching the bar. The next second an apparition appeared in the entrance, standing stock still, surveying the scene, and grinning when every eye – with the exception of Boggis's – turned in its direction.

'Why,' it said in a deep Southern States drawl, 'if this isn't just the sweetest little public house in the whole wide world.'

The owner of the voice, a short, small and somewhat plain-of-feature black man, wearing the most wonderful cape, fully lined in red, together with a pair of matching trousers and pink handmade shoes, stood posing in the doorway, waiting for every eye to turn in his direction. For some reason Nick was reminded of Sammy Davis Jr whom he had seen in films during his childhood.

'Can I have your autograph?' shouted one of the rough trade round by the fruit machines.

'Why most certainly you can,' replied the newcomer, and, with a flourish of his cape, he produced a pen and crossed over to where the other lounged in ancient jeans and a stained T-shirt.

Startled, the youth said, 'Are you famous then?'

'Allow me to give you my card,' said the American, producing one and simultaneously writing his name on the back of a beer mat. 'You see, I am Gerry Harlington.'

'Who?' whispered Kasper.

Nick looked puzzled. 'I don't know except that I've heard he's new in the village. Perhaps he is something in films.'

But Gerry had spied them whispering and, inclining his head graciously to the bewildered youth, advanced upon them, his hand held out.

'Gentlemen, will you do me the honour of letting me buy you a drink?'

'How kind of you,' answered Nick, shaking it. 'But let me introduce myself. I am the vicar of the parish, Nicholas Lawrence. And this is one of our local doctors, Kasper Rudniski.'

Gerry bowed. 'My pleasure. It is an honour to meet two such distinguished residents of my new abode. Now, what can I get you?'

They told him and while Gerry was at the bar Kasper muttered, 'Where has he come from?'

'I don't know but I am about to find out,' Nick answered as the new arrival came back with a bottle of champagne held high, a girl following behind with three glasses.

'Thought I'd forget your order and get a little something for a celebration,' said Gerry with an apologetic smile. He stared at Kasper long and hard before taking his seat. 'You really ought to be in pictures, pal. As I said to Tom Cruise the other day, "New talent is getting so hard to find. What's happened to all the good lookin' fellas?"'

'And what did he answer?' Kasper asked curiously.

'He put his arm round my shoulders and stated, "Wherever they are, you'll find 'em, Gerry."'

There was a slightly uncomfortable silence as nobody was quite sure whether to believe him or not. Then Nick asked, 'Where have you moved in to?'

'I've bought Abbot's Manor. It's been up for sale for a while but it's a great piece of real estate and I just had to have it.'

There was a stunned silence as the vicar and the doctor exchanged a glance. The house that the American had just mentioned had originally been built in medieval times and was in fact still fully moated. There was a distant view of it from the hill at Speckled Wood. It had been practically everybody's dream to buy it and when old Colonel Astaire had died and left the place to a nephew who had swiftly put the ancient dwelling up for sale, there had been a few murmurs of interest. But the price had been prohibitive; just over a million pounds in fact. Gerry Harlington must indeed be a man of resources.

'I take it you are in films?' asked Kasper directly.

Gerry smiled kindly and poured three glasses of The Great House's best champagne. 'Well, cheers people – as you say in England.' He drew in a breath and sighed. 'By God, I love this place. I tell you your little old village of Lakehurst beats New

York, LA, Vegas – remind me to tell you of the time I played there – Norleans, you name 'em. This is the life, here. Where a man can breathe the pure fresh air like the good God intended.' Nick and Kasper stared at him, speechless. From his corner Jack Boggis let out an audible laugh and Gerry immediately turned towards him.

'Why, good evening, sir. I'm afraid I didn't see you stuck away in your nook. Allow me to introduce myself. Gerry Harlington, at your service.'

Boggis glared, said, 'Evening,' and returned to his paper.

Gerry continued, either obtuse or courageous, 'That must be a mighty fine newspaper that you have there.'

Jack slapped it with his hand and said, 'The *Telegraph*. Greatest newspaper there is.'

'That's a matter of opinion,' Nick answered.

'Well, you show me a finer. That *Guardian* rubbish is full of grammatical errors.'

For no reason the vicar felt angry. 'As a matter of fact I think the *Guardian* is well written and extremely informative. I much prefer it to the others.'

'Left-wing rubbish,' said Boggis nastily.

'Now, now, sir,' answered Gerry. 'I had no wish to cause an argument. Come and have a glass of champagne with us.'

'No thanks, I'll stick to beer,' said Jack as affably as was possible for him and returned to the newspaper.

Gerry rolled his eyes upward, showing a great deal of white and mouthed, 'Oh my,' spreading his neat black hands in a gesture of amused despair. He leant back in his chair. 'Well now, people,' he continued, 'let me propose a toast. To England.'

Nick and Kasper raised their glasses and the vicar thought longingly of his early night – but no chance.

Gerry was speaking. 'I like you two boys and I feel certain that question marks are running round in your minds about me even while we speak. So I'm going to tell you my life story and how I got to where I am today. But before I start I want you to realize one thing.' He fixed them with eyes black as coal in the snow. 'I did not choose the theatre. No sir. The theatre chose me.'

The vicar thought that might be quite an apt way of describing any calling but did not dare say a word.

The story unfolded like a bad film, plodding onwards, scene by boring scene. First there was the little black baby born to an unhappy mother – he was her eleventh child – 'And she didn't want no more children to raise single-handed, I can tell you.' Naturally enough, she wept bitter tears when the infant was laid in her arms.

The birth took place in a log cabin – where else? And, predictably, the whereabouts of the sire of this brood were somewhat hazy. Next, the father dramatically reappears but dies in a terrible accident, once more Nick was not sure exactly what happened and how. Then a ne'er-do-well uncle adopts the little boy and takes him to somewhere called Norleans.

Kasper had glanced helplessly at Nick at this stage of the proceedings and the vicar had mouthed the words 'New Orleans'. Kasper had smiled gratefully.

And it was in this strangely named town that the theatre had done its calling. For Uncle Woody was a professional entertainer and somehow or other wove the youthful Gerry into his act. The rest of the tale was predictable enough. Soon the young Harlington was starring on Broadway, then Hollywood called and he was into the big, big time.

'I tell you, gentlemen, that I was on a par with Sammy Davis Jr – even more so, though later of course – but on this side of the pond I would hardly be recognized. You see, I signed a contract to do two films about the Wasp Man . . .'

Nick and Kasper looked at him blankly.

'Well, they were such a smash hit in the States that I was asked to do several more – *Return of the Wasp Man* and *Son of the Wasp Man Strikes Back* being two of them. Reverend, Doctor, I was trapped in the Wasp Man's persona. What was I to do? I disappeared for a month or two – went to Vegas actually – and returned to Tinseltown as a film director. Well, could you blame me? I mean, what would you have done?'

Kasper asked timidly, 'Who exactly was Wasp Man? Forgive me, but I am Polish and do not know these things.'

Gerry gave a smile. 'Of course, I quite understand. Things are very primitive in your country. The Wasp Man was a hip-hop dancer with a hidden secret weapon. One sting from him was lethal. You see he was stung within minutes of his birth and it left him with this legacy.'

'Of hip-hop dancing?' asked Nick innocently.

'No,' answered Gerry, just a shade nastily. 'Of having this murderous sting.'

'Golly!' Nick answered, while Kasper looked very po-faced.

Gerry rambled on regardless. 'When I returned I decided to make films for television not the big screen. So I directed a long-running soap opera called *The Fortune*. It was a smash hit. A family saga with all the usual complications. You know the kind of thing.'

'I believe I saw an episode once in Poland. It had subtitles and was shown very late at night.'

'Did you enjoy it?' asked Gerry eagerly.

Kasper shook his head mournfully. 'Unfortunately I fell asleep.'

'It wasn't shown over here?' asked Nick.

'No. Too sexy, I reckon. Not quite British, you know.'

There was no answer to that so the conversation came to rather an awkward halt. Gerry drained his glass and looked at his Rolex.

'Well, guys, I must fly. It really has been an enormous pleasure. I intend to plunge into village life with a vengeance.' He stood up and pumped the vicar's hand. 'Toodle-oo, see you in church as they say. Bye, Doc.'

And he was gone. Kasper and Nick gazed at the door, then stared at one another, speechless.

'Oh dear,' said Nick.

'What are you thinking?'

'I wonder how the village will take to Wasp Man.'

Kasper shrugged eloquently. 'That we'll just have to wait and see.'

TWO

True to his word, Gerry Harlington made a spectacular entrance into church, waiting until the last possible second before appearing, then making a slow progress up the central aisle, looking both to his right and left and nodding graciously, before taking a seat in the front pew. All but the very elderly stared in amazement and a positive buzz of 'Who is that?' was only hushed by the start of the holy procession. Nick, having taken his seat before the altar, was amused to see that for this occasion Gerry was wearing a soft suede suit in a colour that the vicar could only think of as pink champagne. Beneath it he wore a purple shirt, open at the neck, displaying a vivid gold chain nestling amongst the greying chestal hair.

Afterwards Nick stood outside the ancient church, shaking hands and greeting his parishioners. Further down the steps Gerry had taken up a place in the middle of the path and was stopping everyone who passed him with a brilliant smile and a positive broadside of goodwill. Most of the inhabitants of Lakehurst looked embarrassed, muttered a hasty greeting, and hurried quickly on. But to his surprise Nick saw that Mrs Ivy Bagshot, chairwoman of the local Women's Institute, had actually stopped and was engaging Harlington in an animated conversation. Even though Nick was conversing with an elderly churchgoer at the time he, rather naughtily, strained his ears.

'. . . I knew you were in showbusiness, lady. You have that look about you.'

Mrs Bagshot's claim to the stage had been limited to playing an ageing principal boy in the WI's annual pantomime production, the reason being that she had the longest legs. The fact that facially she had a certain resemblance to a parrot had not come into consideration.

Nick hastily said farewell to the last of the congregation and turned towards Gerry.

'Mr Harlington, I was delighted to see you in church. I heard you singing the hymns with gusto.'

'I was trained vocally, Vicar. I had to sing in the Wasp Man pictures.'

'You were in films?' interrupted Ivy, impressed.

'I certainly was, ma'am. In fact at one time I was the toast of Hollywood.'

Unbelievably Mrs Bagshot swallowed it.

'How very interesting.'

Gerry bowed. 'Most kind, I'm sure. Could I buy you a drink, ma'am? Do you have a spare half-hour?'

Ivy looked at her watch, a gold one on a thin strap. 'Well,

I . . .' She glanced at the vicar as if for approval but he kept his face expressionless. 'I really ought to be getting back.'

'Oh, come now. Surely you can spare half an hour.'

'Oh, very well,' said Ivy capitulating.

The last view that Nick had of them was as they headed purposefully towards The Great House.

As it was not yet one o'clock the public house was relatively empty and Gerry quickly found a small table and seated Ivy at it with a great show of courtly old-world Southern manners.

'What can I get you to drink, ma'am?'

'A sweet sherry, if you please.'

'Coming up.'

He went to the bar and returned a few minutes later with a schooner full of a deep-brown liquid and a large Jack Daniels on the rocks. Taking a seat opposite her, he said, 'May I have the pleasure of knowing your name?'

'Ivy Bagshot,' she answered, her glasses misting slightly.

'Gerry Harlington, at your service. May I say that your name is most becoming, Miss Bagshot.'

'Mrs.'

'Of course. How could I think that an attractive woman like you could have slipped through the net.'

'Are you married, Mr Harlington?'

'Yes,' Gerry answered, somewhat surprisingly. 'But my wife is a regular homebody. She's never happier than when she's in the garden – or polishing something. Of course, we're looking for a cleaner but meanwhile she has Abbot's Manor to care for all by herself.'

'You live there? In the moated manor?' asked Ivy, clearly impressed.

'Yeah. And you know the reason why I temporarily left America and came to England, Mrs Bagshot?'

'No.'

'I want to make a documentary on village life. The good, the bad and the ugly. Every aspect of what goes on behind the respectable facade.'

'Oh goodness! Do you direct for television then?'

'Sure. I directed one of the most popular soaps on US TV.

And I have also had a most interesting career in films. Let me tell you about it – that is if you would like to hear.'

'Oh yes, I would. Very much.'

Nearly an hour later, cheeks flushed from too much sherry, Ivy was sitting agog, listening to the exploits of the Wasp Man. She even tittered broad-mindedly at the mention of a hip-hop dancer.

'Can you really do that, Mr Harlington? I mean dance in that fashion?'

'Lady, I can do anything when it comes to the stage. I am what you Brits would call a good all-rounder. And what about you? What parts have you played?'

'Nothing in your league, I'm afraid. I usually get cast as principal boy in the local village pantomime. But I was to have been the Lady Marguerite Beau de Grave – amongst other things – but, alas, that is now not to be.'

'Why is that? I don't understand.'

'Do you really want to hear about it? I mean, it's all local stuff.'

Gerry narrowed his eyes. 'Mrs Bagshot, everything is of interest to me. Yes, siree.'

'Well, there is a much larger village than ours about ten miles away. It's called Oakbridge. Perhaps you've heard of it?' Gerry shook his head. 'Anyway they have quite a thriving dramatic society and, of course, they have – had – Mr Merryfield.'

'Who he?'

'Well, he was a sort of white version of you,' Ivy babbled on tactlessly. 'He had been an actor, director, writer, everything. He just happened to retire to Oakbridge . . .'

'He was an elderly man then?'

'Oh yes, well into his seventies. Not a bit like you really,' she added, sensing that Gerry was fractionally put out.

'I'm pleased to hear that, Mrs Bagshot. Do go on.'

'Well, he had conceived the idea of writing the script for a Son et Lumière to be performed at Fulke Castle.'

'I'm sorry, ma'am, I don't know where that is. But first, would you like another sherry? I see that your glass is empty.'

Ivy giggled, something she hadn't done for years. 'Well, I oughtn't to.'

'Oh come on, lady. You've had hardly anything.'

Ivy fished in her small handbag and produced an even smaller purse. 'It's my turn but I would rather that you went to the bar.' She handed him a ten-pound note which he was busy refusing when at that moment the door opened and the vicar, dressed in jeans and a sweater, appeared. 'Oh Vicar,' Ivy called gaily. 'What are you having? It's my round.'

Thinking that wonders would never cease, Nick walked over to her table. 'Well, thank you very much, Mrs Bagshot. I'll have a pint of Harvey's please. May I join you?'

She nodded and he sat down and looked round. Jack Boggis was in his usual place, back to the throng, facing the wall, nose in the paper, contributing nothing. Giles Fielding was sitting at the bar, eyeing up Gerry, as were a great many of the other regulars. Kasper had been invited out to lunch and was conspicuous by his non-appearance. In fact, other than for the absence of the doctor, things were very much as normal.

The door of The Great House opened once again and in walked Madisson, a very tall, very thin, very blonde girl who had opened a beauty parlour some six doors up from the church. She sailed up to the bar and stood next to Gerry, who glanced at her with a great deal of admiration.

Nick waited for the line, 'Say, honey, you ought to be in pictures,' and was almost relieved when out it came.

Madisson looked Gerry up and down with a cool regard. 'No thanks, I'm quite happy with my life.'

'But, darling, you could be a big star.'

'Get you!' she said, and went to join her friends who were sitting at a table nearby.

Looking slightly crestfallen, Gerry came back with the drinks and turned on Ivy Bagshot a beaming smile. 'Now, Mrs B., you were telling me about the adventures of Mr Merryfield.'

The vicar came in on the conversation. 'Wasn't that the poor chap from Oakbridge who died recently?'

Mrs Bagshot looked earnest. 'Oh yes, indeed. And as I was telling Mr Harlington he has left the Odds in a state of confusion.'

'Odds?' Nick repeated, puzzled.

'Yes. The Oakbridge Dramatists and Dramatic Society.'

Nick thought this title was rather overdoing things but said nothing and prepared to listen as Ivy launched into her tale.

'He'd written the script for and was going to direct a Son et Lumière at Fulke Castle. That is a stately home about twelve miles away in the middle of the countryside, Mr Harlington. Anyway, it was such a big cast that they asked the WI if they could provide any actresses to help them out. Naturally I stepped forward as did Mrs Howes and Mrs Emms. But, of course, it was men they were desperately short of. And now, as fate would have it, the director himself.'

'But surely he had an assistant?' This from Nick.

'Well, yes. Young Oswald Souter, who applied for the position in order to learn how to direct. In other words, I fear he is a trifle youthful and inexperienced to take over such a huge project.'

Nick nodded and Gerry sucked his teeth audibly.

'Tell me about Fulke Castle.'

Mrs Bagshot sipped her sherry. 'Well, in parts it goes back to 1067, so it was built right after the Norman invasion, though there have been tons of additions since. The part that is lived in is mainly Victorian. But it's all open to the public.'

'So it's not National Trust?' asked Nick.

'No, believe it or not it is still in the hands of the original family, though goodness alone knows how. The present owner is Sir Rufus Beaudegrave, his ancestor having come over with William the Conqueror. Anyway, he lets the castle out for films and television – that sort of thing – and has hordes of people poring over the staterooms and so on, and in this way somehow manages to keep the place going.'

'So was he hiring it out to the Odds?'

'Yes, but I believe he gave them a cut rate because Mr Merryfield was going to tell its story – and a very fascinating one it was too – but with actors and horses and dogs and sound and light. Oh, it was going to have been so wonderful.'

And Mrs Bagshot's eyes, big behind their glasses, suddenly welled with tears.

Gerry spoke. 'Come now, ma'am, there's no need for that. Wasp Man to the rescue.'

She and Nick stared at him blankly.

'While you were speaking I felt the pull of your old Castle

Fulke. I shall be happy to offer my services as director to your friends in Oakbridge. If they'll have me, of course.'

This last was said with a sly expression that reminded Nick of a dog stealing sausages.

Mrs Bagshot's throat flushed scarlet and a tear trickled down and left a rivulet in her powder.

'Oh, would you?' she cried ecstatically, her hands clasping as if in prayer.

'Yes, ma'am, I will. If I may put a new spin on the words, "I didn't call the castle; the castle called me". Now you just go home and phone those Oakbridge oddities and tell them that help is at hand. Give them my professional details and I'll wait to get the OK.'

Inwardly Nick shuddered at the thought of the Wasp Man let loose on something as ancient and as precious as Fulke Castle but he kept quiet and concentrated his mind on what he was having for lunch instead.

That night, when evensong was over and Nick was just relaxing, putting his feet up and attempting a brute of a crossword in one of the Sunday papers, there was a ring at the front door. Pulling a face at Radetsky, who gave him a look of pure disapproval in return, he went to answer it and was surprised to see a strange young woman standing there. She gave him a big apologetic smile.

'Good evening, Reverend Lawrence, I'm so sorry to disturb you and I do apologize for calling so late.'

'How can I help you?' he said, opening the door and ushering her into the hall.

'Well, it's a bit of a delicate matter.'

Inwardly Nick sighed, wondering what was coming next. Ahead of him the girl walked into the living room and pulled a beret from her head so that a great mass of crocus-coloured hair came tumbling round her shoulders. She smiled once more.

'First I think I'd better introduce myself. I'm Jonquil Charmwood.'

'Is that really your name?' Nick said.

'Yes. Why?'

'It's just that it's so unusual.'

She laughed. 'I'm glad you like it.'

'I do. Very much. Now what can I do for you, Miss Charmwood?'

He motioned her to a chair and as she sat down there was a sudden creak of floorboards from above. They both looked up.

'William,' said Nick with a grin. 'He's my resident ghost. Nice old fellow. Wouldn't hurt a fly.'

'Really? I've always wanted to meet a ghost. Do you see him?'

'Very occasionally. But anyway, you haven't come here to talk about him I take it.'

'No. It's actually about the Son et Lumière at Fulke Castle.'

'Not trouble already?' Nick said without thinking.

'No, not really. You know, of course, that Mr Merryfield died of a sudden heart attack. Well, the show was due to be cancelled and then Mrs Bagshot of Lakehurst rang the secretary of Odds – me – and said that this most marvellous actor and director had recently moved into the village and was offering to save the day.'

'Yes, it's true enough.'

'Do you think he's capable of doing it?'

Nick sat down opposite her and decided to be honest. 'Look, I've only met the man twice but he has had a career in Hollywood out of which he must have made a great deal of money because the house he bought, which is just outside Lakehurst by the way, was on the market for a considerable fortune. As to his talents, I really can't say. I've never seen any of his films or any of his television series so it's not possible for me to comment. I'm sorry.'

'Oh dear,' said Jonquil, and shook her head from side to side so that her lively hair flew. 'Well, we'll just have to judge for ourselves I suppose. He's coming along to the next rehearsal.'

'That will be your chance then.'

'Yes, it will.' She stood up. 'Thank you so much, Vicar.'

He rose as well. 'I'm sorry I couldn't be of more help.'

Jonquil made her way to the front door. 'It's a lovely place you have here,' she said, looking around.

'Yes, I like it. You must come and see it in the daylight.'

Why did I just say that? He asked himself.

'Thank you, I will,' she answered, and disappeared into the street.

There was a thump on the landing.

'Glad you approve, William,' the vicar called, and went back to his crossword.

THREE

t was not destined to be a peaceful evening. At 10.30, just as Nick was preparing to go to bed, the telephone rang again. This time it was Ivy, definitely tipsy and slurring her words.

'Hello, Father Nick, hello.'

Oh really! thought Nick, having been brought up to believe that phoning anyone after nine was rude.

'I just thought I'd give you a little call to thank you for introducing me to Mr Harlington.'

'Well, I hardly . . .'

'And for rescuing the Son et Lumière. You truly are a man of miracles.'

To argue that it had been absolutely nothing to do with him would have been futile. Ivy Bagshot, pillar of the WI and unused to alcohol as she was, was plain old-fashioned drunk.

'Thank you,' said Nick, and waited.

'Are you there, Vicar?'

'Yes, I'm here, Mrs Bagshot. Was there something else?'

'One small tiny favour.'

Nick's heart sank. 'What might that be?'

'The Odds are extremely short of men, Father. I mean now that the show is proceeding . . .' But what if it doesn't, thought Nick, remembering Jonquil Charmwood's visit.

'. . . we shall need some strong men and true.' Mrs Bagshot gave a muted hiccough. 'So I wondered if you, Father Nick . . .'

'I'm sorry to disappoint you but I couldn't possibly take on anything extra at the moment,' the vicar answered firmly.

'Oh dear me, are you sure?'

'Certain.'

'But Father . . .'

'Would you believe there is someone knocking at my door,'

lied Nick desperately. 'I really will have to go. Goodnight, Mrs Bagshot.'

He put the receiver down, feeling pale, and went to the drinks cupboard and poured himself a small gin and tonic which he consumed with much enjoyment. Then he went to bed.

The committee of the Oakbridge Dramatists and Dramatic Society was in full spate, shouting at one another loudly while the chairman, a rather handsome and beautifully spoken man who modelled himself on Donald Sinden, was banging on the table with the palm of his hand and saying, 'One at a time, please. One at a time.' To which they paid no attention whatsoever.

The person with the loudest voice, a booming middle-aged man with erstwhile matinee-idol looks, was saying in a well-bred drawl, 'But dammit all, we don't know anything about the fella. He comes in here with some cock-and-bull story about playing Ant Man and expects us to hand him a major production on a plate.'

'But if we don't we're sunk,' said an enormous blonde woman with equally enormous locks, hanging to her waist and done in a style dating back to the sixties and Farrah Fawcett. 'I mean, it will be too much for young Oswald and that's for sure.'

'Can't Mrs Wrigglesworth help him?' said a timid-looking woman with mousey hair scraped back and a shining, earnest face to which make-up had never been introduced.

'I know she has directed for us before but she's far too busy with her many other interests,' retorted the big blonde, whose name was Annette Muffat.

'I think we'll have to take a chance on this Gerry fellow. I mean, it's either that or we cancel the whole thing,' said the Oakbridge chiropodist, who was small and purposeful and, apparently, a wizard with verrucas.

'I quite agree,' said Jonquil Charmwood, raising her voice. She was secretary of the Odds. 'I mean, what other alternative have we?'

The chairman at last managed to speak. His voice was huge; a vast, mellifluent thing of which he was inordinately proud. He always captured the big Shakespearean roles and was excessively pleased with his recent Prospero. Almost as pleased as he was with himself. He was a local solicitor and was charming to his women clients, brusque and mannish with the males. His name was Paul Silas which looked very good printed on a theatrical programme, in his opinion anyway.

'It seems to me, as there is obviously disagreement in the ranks, that I must get a feel for what the majority wish. I shall put it to you one by one and I would request that the rest of you remain silent.' He turned to Jonquil. 'Madam Secretary, what is your feeling about employing this Harlington fellow?'

'Well I don't think he's ideal but what other alternative have we? I mean the show is so advanced. The commentary has been recorded by Rafael Devine, who gave his services free of charge as a favour to poor Ben Merryfield. I mean, what would he say if we suddenly pulled out?'

Rafael Devine was a long-established actor, a National Theatre player and star of both television and films. Paul Silas personally felt that Devine's work was inferior to his own but had never publicly voiced such a thought.

'Then I take it we would have an aye vote from you?'

'Yes,' said Jonquil. 'We're too far gone to draw back.'

Paul turned to the plain girl. 'And what about you, Madam Treasurer? How would you vote?'

She wavered, turning her make-up-less face towards Annette, who glowered at her.

'I'm not sure,' she said meekly.

'Oh don't be so wet,' said Meg Alexander, who was married to the fading matinee idol and seemed engaged with him on a path of running the whole society. 'Vote no.'

'No,' said the poor wretch then went bright red.

'I see,' said Paul deeply. He turned to the other members of the committee. 'And what are your wishes, Madam Vice Chairman?'

'Oh, don't be so pompous,' said the fair-haired woman to whom he was speaking. She had at one time done some paid work in the theatre and was reverentially referred to as an 'ex-professional' by the other members of the drama group. 'I say yes. If this American man turns out to be a turd we'll just ignore him. But we need someone to pull the show together.'

'Hear, hear,' put in the Oakbridge chiropodist whose name was Barry Beardsley.

'I take it from that that you are in favour of employing Mr Harlington?'

'Well, it's hardly employing as he is offering his services. But, yes, I would agree to being directed by King Kong as long as we get this bloody Son et Lumière on.'

The votes having been taken it turned out that they were tied, four in favour and four against using the services of the Wasp Man. It was left to the chairman to give his casting vote.

Paul Silas sunk his chin into his hand, hoping that he looked like Michael Gambon in a thoughtful posture, and ran his brilliant brown eyes over the assembled committee. They came to rest warmly on Jonquil who hastily gazed in the other direction. He spoke.

'I see that it is beholden upon me . . .'

'Oh get on with it.' This from the Vice Chairman, Estelle Yeoman, who did not suffer fools gladly.

'To give my casting vote. And though I do so with some trepidation . . .'

Estelle rolled her eyes at Jonquil, who grinned.

'. . . I have come down on that which I believe will be of benefit to the whole society. I have, after much thought, decided in favour of Mr Harlington.'

'Thank God for that,' said Annette loudly and got to her feet. 'Well, I'm off to The Royal Oak. Who's coming with me?'

'I will,' said Robin Green, a hairy-faced individual of indeterminate age who always insisted, regardless of the weather, on wearing a pair of knee-length khaki shorts and leather sandals.

'Oh dear,' she answered, but nonetheless left the building with him.

Jonquil stood up. 'Well, I'm off.'

Paul gave her what he considered to be a captivating smile. 'Can I buy you a drink, my dear?'

She hesitated, then the Oakbridge footman spoke up. 'Come on, Jonquil. I'll protect you from strange men.'

Paul glared but could find no answer and was left with the job of putting the lights out and locking up. Then he slowly walked round the corner to The Royal Oak to join the others, none of whom were particularly glad to see him.

*   *   *

In the privacy of his study, the medieval walls of which he had hung with full-length photographs of himself in various film roles, Gerry Harlington was sitting at an electric keyboard.

'I gotta tiny longing,' he crooned noisily, the sound reverberating off the stone walls of the magnificent moated manor house in which he now dwelled. 'A longing to be free.'

Satisfied, he repeated the action into several different recording devices, then stood up and paced round the large room, staring at the expensive and in some cases extremely ancient wall hangings which interspersed his photographs and thinking how he would like to tear them down and redecorate the entire place in bright colours. Yet one thing stood in his way, his wife, Mrs Ekaterina Harlington. For all her lack of ambition, the woman had good taste, he had to grant her that. Whistling to himself, Gerry, with a supreme lack of regard for the environment and expense, left the room with all lights blazing and made his way upstairs.

If truth be told he didn't like walking round Abbot's Manor in the half-light. The house was terribly old, some of it having been built in the late thirteenth century. Just to add to its generally spooky atmosphere there had originally been a monastery on the site which had fallen into disrepair and the ruins of which had been built over by one William de Tillburgh in 1287. Gerry Harlington might have played Wasp Man – 'Kill with a Sting' – but he firmly believed in the supernatural and always hated walking down the long corridor that led to the master bedroom at the end.

He did so now with an air of nonchalance but jumped and whipped round, terrified, when a floorboard creaked behind him.

Ekaterina was sitting up in bed, reading a copy of *Vogue*. She held it in one elegantly manicured hand while the other held a glass of vodka and tonic, which she was sipping through a straw with a loop in it. She looked up as Gerry entered.

'Oh, it's you. How did you get on?'

'What a load of merchant bankers,' he answered, having just heard the phrase that very evening from Barry Beardsley, voiced during Gerry's interview by the Odds committee.

'What?' asked Ekaterina, putting down her magazine.

'It's an English expression. I think it means wankers. Cockney rhyming slang, you know.'

'Oh.'

Ekaterina had already lost interest and picked up *Vogue* once more.

She was the daughter of a Russian oligarch, her grandfather being a peasant from Omsk who had discovered oil on his land and become incredibly rich as a result. Poorly educated but packed full of native cunning, he had invested wisely and thus his son, Grigori – Ekaterina's father – had become one of the wealthiest men in the world and had emigrated to Britain where he had invested in a football club. Yet money can't buy good health, as the saying goes. At the height of his powers, with six houses in the United Kingdom, four in the United States, and three in Russia, to say nothing of a fleet of luxury yachts, planes and helicopters, he had been struck down by terminal cancer and had died at the age of fifty-six.

He had only had one child, his daughter, with whom he had fallen out many years before. Ekaterina had moved with him to America and there she had become involved with a crowd of dope-smoking left-wing poets, who lay on couches, listening to one of their number read absurd poems aloud. Ekaterina, who had inherited her grandfather's foxlike intelligence, soon got bored with this and used her father's allowance to drift off to Hollywood where she had some idle notion of getting into films. But she had not acknowledged one thing – her incredible ugliness. She was stick thin, had a pronounced squint and an enormous hooked nose, while her hair simply hung in a mouse-coloured straggle.

It was at this stage of her life that she met Gerry Harlington, a poorly paid actor starring in a series of low-budget films about wasps. She thought it rather daring to be dated by a young black actor, particularly one who seemed absolutely smitten with her, for she, innocent abroad, had no idea that he had done some research into her surname. They were married in Las Vegas and set up home in a small flat in downtown Los Angeles. And it was there that she received the news that her father had died and that she was his sole heiress.

'So how did you get on with that acting crowd?' she asked, looking up from *Vogue* once more.

'They begged me to direct them, that's all I can say.'

'And will you?'

'I'll think about it,' Gerry answered offhandedly, going into the glorious bathroom that was the one alteration to the building that Ekaterina had allowed.

She heard him start to run the shower, then secretly looked up at the mirror above the bed that Gerry had insisted they install. A Slavonic but beautiful face looked back at her and Ekaterina smiled at it. She had spent literally millions of dollars on plastic surgery: rhinoplasty, opting for a nose like Julia Roberts; implants put into her meagre breasts; her jaw reduced and her eyes lengthened. She had got rid of her squint by means of an operation in a Swiss clinic. Then she had consulted a leading hair stylist. She had completely reinvented herself and her photograph frequently appeared in gossip columns and also in *The Sunday Times Rich List*. And wherever she went she made an impact, an impact which did not include her husband for she preferred to appear in public on her own. But for now, moved into this fabulous house in a remote part of Sussex, she had decided to play along with being the quiet-little-wife-at-home image that he was clearly creating for her. For the time being, anyway.

Gerry came out of the shower wrapped in a red bath towel and posed before a cheval looking-glass. He flexed his muscles and made the sound of a wasp in flight. Ekaterina yawned and said, 'What was that phone call you had earlier?'

'What phone call?'

'The one that came through about nine? It rang up here but I didn't answer it.'

'Oh that.' Gerry looked bored. 'It was just from the chairman of the drama group. Apparently I was unanimously chosen to direct this little Son et Lumière. My God, it sounds dull as doggie's do-dos. I think it should be set to music. In fact I've already got one or two ideas.'

'Fascinating,' said Ekaterina, yawned again, and picked up *Vogue*.

FOUR

Nick was somewhat surprised to receive a letter a couple of days later with a florid crest on the letterhead and the address Abbot's Manor, Speckled Wood, printed below. It was written in rather a childish hand using a blue felt-tipped pen and had the odd grammatical error. On closer examination the crest was revealed to be a black lion rampant garnished with vivid yellow, sporting two tails and a set of nasty-looking red claws, being viciously attacked by a wasp. The words Vespula Homo in ancient script were written beneath. Nick smiled and shook his head, sipping his coffee.

'Dear Vicar,' he read aloud. 'Seems as how I've been drummed in to this Son et Lumière thing. Believe me I tried to say no but the guys at Oakbridge twisted my arm, as the proverb goes.' Nick raised an amused eyebrow. 'Anyway, this is an apology for my not throwing myself into village activities as I said I would but my time will be taken up, as you can imagine. By the way, the men I saw at rehearsal the other night were either senile or senseless. Any chance of you joining us? Sincerely yours, Gerry Harlington.'

The idea that it might be rather fun to do – provided that there was no script to learn – suddenly struck Nick strongly. After all, he asked himself, why not? He reached over and looked in his diary for the month ahead. Admittedly there were a few evening engagements, parochial meetings mainly and one he particularly enjoyed, meeting the friends of the church and discussing with them the various ways of raising money through social events. But other than for those it was clear. On an impulse he went to the telephone and dialled the number printed beneath the letter-head. Somewhat to his surprise a woman's voice answered. He put on his formal mode.

'Hello. Would it be possible to speak to Mr Harlington please.'

'I am afraid he is out at the moment. Who is calling please?'

There was a subtle but definite accent underlying the way she spoke.

'This is the vicar of Lakehurst. Are you his secretary?'

She laughed a fraction cynically. 'Yes, you could call me that I suppose. Actually I'm his wife.'

Nick nearly dropped the receiver. 'Good gracious. I'm so sorry. I . . .' He stopped himself from saying 'I didn't know he had one' and instead said, 'I'm delighted to make your acquaintance.'

'But we haven't met,' Ekaterina pointed out.

The vicar laughed to hide his embarrassment. 'I hope that will be swiftly remedied.'

'I hope so too. Anyway, he's not here. Can I take a message?'

'Yes. You can tell him that I've decided to be in the Son et Lumière as long as I don't have to say anything.'

'No, that you will not have to do. It has already been pre-recorded by Rafael Devine.'

'My goodness. How did the Oakbridge people persuade him to do that?'

'I think it was something concerning the man who died. But I truly don't know any more.'

'Well, thank you anyway. Can you ask your husband to ring me when he gets back?'

'Of course.'

There was a slight pause, then Nick said, 'Any hope of seeing you in church?'

'I am afraid not. I will go to the Russian Orthodox in London if I feel the need.'

'Oh, I see. Well, thank you for your help. I do hope we can meet one day.'

Ekaterina answered, 'I should like that.' Then she unexpectedly added, 'Why not today? Gerry has gone somewhere or other. Let me take you to lunch.'

'Well, I . . .'

'Come now, Vicar. I know no one here. It would be kind of you to say yes.'

'Very well. Shall we say The Great House at one o'clock.'

'I shall be there.'

Nick arrived ten minutes early and ordered himself a lime and soda, then found a table for two and sat at it. Jack Boggis was a few feet away but did not look up as the vicar approached. For some contrary reason Nick found himself saying, 'Hello, Jack,' in a loud voice.

The Yorkshireman removed his nose from the *Daily Telegraph*. He looked slightly annoyed.

'Morning, Vicar.'

'I trust you are keeping well.'

'I've been better, I've been worse.'

'I'm delighted to hear it.'

There was a tap on Nick's shoulder and he looked up and into the face of an absolutely spectacular blonde. Enormously wide-set eyes, a smoky mysterious blue, set amongst voluminous eyelashes – could they really be real? – gazed frankly into his. The rest of the features were perfect – a triumph of the surgeon's art, Nick found himself thinking. A beautiful nose, a chiselled jawline, everything about the woman shouted money, including the designer casuals that she was wearing. A wave of expensive perfume hit his nostrils as he scrambled to his feet.

'Mrs Harlington?' he asked.

'Just call me Ekaterina,' she answered, and sat down gracefully opposite him.

The effect on Jack Boggis was amazing. He actually lowered the *Daily Telegraph* and his face suffused a dull shade of trodden grape.

'Does that include me?' he said with an attempt at a manly laugh.

She looked him up and down coolly. 'If you wish,' she replied, and shrugged a casual shoulder. Nick thought that she was one of the most elegant creatures he had seen in years.

It was out before he could control the words. 'Are you really married to Gerry Harlington?' he said.

'Yes. Why?'

'I don't know. It's just that the two of you are quite different.'

She shrugged again. 'Why do we have to be alike? What would be the point of that?'

Nick looked penitent. 'Forgive me. I am speaking out of turn.'

Boggis butted in. 'So you're new to our village, little lady?'

She regarded him unsmilingly. 'Yes. We moved into Abbot's Manor a week ago. Why?'

'Because if you want someone to show you round, I'm your man.'

'Perhaps you could direct me to the best gymnasium in the area. I'm looking for a personal trainer.'

'Hoh, hoh,' chortled Jack. 'I'd volunteer if I were a few years younger.'

Ekaterina's expression did not change. 'I used to belong to The Sports Club in LA. It's on Wilshire Boulevard. Do you know it?'

The vicar interposed. 'It sounds very grand but I don't think we've anything to match that round here. I'd try Brighton. The only thing is it's quite a way.'

For the first time Ekaterina smiled. 'That doesn't worry me. I will take your advice. Thank you.' She picked up a menu. 'Now then, what would you like to eat?'

An hour later and Nick found himself still in her company. She was one of those women who had the knack of drawing a great deal of information from her associate whilst imparting little about herself. All he had been able to ascertain was that she had been born in Russia but had gone to America as a teenager and there met Gerry. He, on the other hand, was discussing the parish, his comfortable but eccentric home, and his spur-of-the-moment decision to take part in the Son et Lumière. He had even mentioned that he owned a cat.

Ekaterina pursed her beautiful lips – surely they had been enhanced in some magical way – and said, 'I don't know how Gerry is going to get on with that dramatic society.'

'Why do you say that?'

'Because he is a hip-hop dancer at heart. He likes setting things to music – which he composes himself – and then dancing to it.'

'But surely he won't be able to do that with this production. I mean, it is the history of Fulke Castle.'

Ekaterina rearranged her stunning features. 'Wait and see.'

'Are you going to be in it?' asked Nick hopefully.

'I don't know. I haven't been asked.'

'Well, I think you should.'

'I'll think about it,' she answered.

Despite all the vicar's protestations she insisted on paying for lunch. Aware of Jack Boggis's baggy gaze glinting at him, Nick accepted graciously, then walked out to the car park with her. His eyes nearly popped out of his head when he saw a Bugatti Veyron Super Sports in a dazzling shade of blue standing there.

'Is this yours?' he asked in wonderment.

'Sure,' said Ekaterina, easing her slender shape into the driver's seat.

Rapidly thinking that Gerry Harlington must be in the millionaire league, Nick stared at it.

'I've never seen one before,' he admitted.

'Get in. I'll give you a ride round the countryside.'

'Well, I . . .'

'Oh, just get in. It will give your parishioners something to think about.'

As Nick slid into the incredibly well-upholstered seat he wondered what Mavis Cox would make of it all as Ekaterina accelerated from zero to sixty in a few seconds as they flew down Arrow Street.

It was the first rehearsal and Gerry was bustling with importance. Rustling a sheet of papers he stared round the room and called, 'Quiet please.' The Oakbridge Dramatists and Dramatic Society obediently obeyed, looking at him with expectant eyes.

'Hi, y'all,' he said, projecting his voice to a boom. 'Allow me to introduce myself – to those of you who don't know me already. My name is Gerry Harlington and I – yes, you're right – starred in the Wasp Man films.'

There was a stunned silence. Gerry continued.

'I also directed a soap opera that was just enormous on TV. It was called *The Fortune*. Unfortunately it was not shown here in Britain but any of you who have visited the States will surely have seen it.'

One of the company spoke up. It was Robin Green, dressed in the usual shorts and sandals and speaking through a mass of facial hair.

'Yes, I saw an excerpt in San Francisco. There were a lot of black people driving around in cars. I didn't quite get the gist.'

Gerry laughed gaily. 'Wow, that's tough. Now I want to ask

a question before we start rehearsal. How many of you boys and gals can dance? Hands up please.'

Four girls, including the delectable Jonquil Charmwood, put up a tentative hand. Gerry looked round, twinkling.

'What? No fellas? Say now, can't any of you move?'

Robin Green ventured, 'Well, I can dance a bit.'

Nick, who was attending his very first rehearsal and was not at all sure of himself, said, 'I studied tap dancing when I was at school.'

'Great, we have two of you.'

Paul Silas, the chairman of the society, spoke in beautifully modulated tones. 'Excuse me interrupting, Mr Harlington, but what do you need dancers for? Is it for the Elizabethan Fair scene?'

The Wasp Man looked surprised, then chuckled. 'Why no, sir. I tell you I've read your script through and through and I thought we could liven the whole thing up by setting it to music and introducing a dance number here and there.'

There was a shocked silence and then a groundswell of protest.

'You can't do that,' said an unknown voice from the back.

'Do you realize,' put in Mike Alexander, the man who was dying to take over the entire society, 'that you are dealing with an actual history. The history of Fulke Castle. You can't stick in dances and music. We have all the music we need on the soundtrack which has been recorded by no less a luminary than Rafael Devine.'

'Ah,' said Gerry, looking blank. 'I don't know his work.'

'That is a great pity. He happens to be one of the leading lights of our theatre and is much revered. Indeed, he has made several films that have been shown in the USA and was once nominated for an Oscar.'

'Oh heck, yes, I know who you mean. Didn't he play in *Starlit Heroes*?'

'That was Sir Michael Gambon,' put in the unknown voice sepulchrally.

'Oh well.' Gerry shrugged. 'So, folks, run your show before me. I'll be interested to see what you can do with it.'

He retired to a folding chair he had brought with him which had *Gerry Harlington* written in large letters across the back.

Nick thought, somewhat unkindly, that he had seen chairs just like it advertised in a catalogue on which you could have printed the name of your choice.

The Son et Lumière was set in several scenes, the first of which was the arrival at Fulke Castle by the first Sir Fulke Beau de Grave. From a recorder at the back of the room came the gorgeous voice of Rafael Devine describing the event. Meanwhile, the actors acted out the story in dumbshow, the part of Fulke Beau de Grave being played by Paul Silas. Nick, who was merely a common workman involved in the building scene, was surprised to learn from the commentary that building on the castle had not actually finished until the penultimate year of the reign of Queen Victoria, in 1900.

As the next scene would require a costume change he was not in it and neither was the attractive Jonquil Charmwood. She had greeted Nick as he had entered the room but now they had a chance for a chat.

'Shall we step outside?' she whispered.

But before Nick could so much as nod Gerry had shouted from his corner, 'No conversations during rehearsal, if you please. Those who want to talk can go somewhere else. And that's an order.'

Feeling as if every eye was upon him, Nick slipped out of the door which Jonquil was holding open and into a functional kitchen. They were rehearsing in a large church hall, close to St Matthew's, Oakbridge, a somewhat dreary-looking parish which the vicar was secretly glad had not come his way.

Jonquil broke the silence with two words. 'Oh dear.'

'Yes it was a bit awful.'

'A bit? It was absolutely shocking. How dare he want to set the show to music! And with that glorious soundtrack we've got already. He should be shot.'

'Oh, come now. Gerry's not that bad.'

'He's worse,' Jonquil answered violently. 'I regret that we ever asked him to take over. We should have asked Estelle Yeoman.'

'Who's she?'

'She's the blonde woman playing one of the Ladies Beau de Grave. She's done professional work in her time and she doesn't stand for any nonsense.'

'I wonder why she hasn't spoken up?'

'Don't worry, she will.'

And, just as Jonquil had predicted, Estelle was holding forth in icy tones as they re-entered the rehearsal room.

'Mr Harlington, do you have any concept of English history? To suggest a hip-hop routine during the Elizabethan Fair is absolutely ludicrous. We would be greeted with hails of derisive laughter.'

'I don't quite follow that,' answered Gerry with an attempt at enormous dignity.

'Look, you may have been the star of numerous films which I feel sure were, in their way, enormous successes. But you can't play around with the facts. You truly can't.'

'Not even if it were dressed up as a morris dance?'

'What do you mean, exactly?'

'Well,' said Gerry, with a sly grin, 'just you wait and see.'

Nick left the rehearsal with a welter of mixed feelings. First of all he was completely enraptured by the thought and care that had gone into planning the Son et Lumière. The splendour of the scenes as they would be enacted when they finally moved to Fulke Castle would, he knew, leave the audience gasping. There would be horses, sword fighting, a fall from the battlements, even an Irish wolfhound in the Civil War scene. He also felt a tremendous pleasure at being part of it and despite all the ill feeling that had been obvious in the church hall that night, he was certain that the show could do nothing but triumph. And yet there was a niggling doubt.

If the Wasp Man really were to introduce something entirely irrelevant and in poor taste, what would happen? Could he jeopardize the whole concept which had clearly originally been written by someone with great artistry and flair? The only place in which he could do something as anachronistic as hip-hop dancing would be the Elizabethan Fair scene, which had music playing under the commentary throughout and therefore would give him a window of opportunity.

In his prayers that night the vicar asked most fervently that this depressing possibility would not come to materialize.

FIVE

Ekaterina was lying in the small garden which lay between the main house and the building behind it, the old servants' quarters. The place was a suntrap and despite it being early September she was stretched out on a massage couch wearing a small thong while a handsome masseur applied aromatic oils to her back. She sighed with contentment and said, 'A little higher please, Ricardo.' The masseur obeyed.

He was a typical Italian stallion, rippling muscles, wavy longish black hair, a fact that he played to its fullest extent. He had actually been born in England and had attended Tulse Hill Comprehensive School, his parents running a restaurant in the vicinity of Charing Cross Station. His natural speech was pure South London but he had abandoned this for a broken Italian accent that made young girls feel randy and older women dream. In fact, he considered, as he moved his supple fingers up towards Ekaterina's shoulder blades, it had been his voice that had latterly got him into a rather nasty scrape.

Last month he had had the sack from the Keep Young and Beautiful Spa, where his list of clients had included a certain Mrs Liversedge-Herone, a lady of some sixty years who had practically risen from the massage couch and seduced him – at least that was his story. Unfortunately her husband had found out about their affair and also happened to play golf with one of the directors. Instant dismissal for Ricardo, who had since been freelancing with a fold-up couch in the boot of his car and jars of oils pinched from the spa as a goodbye present to himself.

But now the fates had smiled on him once more. He had been telephoned by a Mrs Harlington and asked if he could come to a remote Sussex village to give her a course of massage. And a little research into who she was had blown him into the stratosphere. He had discovered that her husband was a second-rate actor from America – in his mind Ricardo was already imagining Gerry being dropped like a hot potato – but she was the daughter

of the late Grigori Makarichoff and his sole heir. On his first
visit Ricardo had taken in the glories of the moated manor,
Ekaterina's cars, which had been lined up in the garage on the
near side of the bridge crossing the moat, and finally Ekaterina
herself. He had promptly gone and booked himself a room in
The Great House for an indeterminate stay.

'Could you see to my shoulders, Ricardo? They occasionally
give me pain,' said Ekaterina in her lilting Russian voice.

'It is tension, madam. Something is worrying you,' he
answered, his words oozing Latin charm. 'Ah, the back of your
neck is a knot of anxiety.'

'I wonder why that should be?'

'Only you will know the answer,' Ricardo answered softly,
and kneaded the top of her spine rhythmically.

At precisely that moment Nick Lawrence was crossing the
delightful small bridge which led to the great oak door of
the moated manor. He was on a random parochial visit and,
though he knew that Ekaterina was Russian Orthodox by faith,
had hopes of somehow encouraging her to become part of the
Lakehurst community, though to be honest he could hardly see
her arranging flowers. Or, for that matter, joining the WI. In fact
as he pulled at the long iron lever that worked the bell he could
hardly think of any attractions that the village might offer that
would suit Ekaterina.

There was a long silence after it rang sonorously in the house's
depths and Nick was just about to turn away and recross the
bridge when the front door opened. A young man in a white top
stood there.

'Can I help you?' he asked, his accent extreme Italianate.

'Er, yes. Is Mrs Harlington in?'

'She is presently getting dressed.' At the look of surprise on
the vicar's face, Ricardo added, 'I have just given her a massage.'

'Oh. Oh, I see. Well I was only here on a parochial call. I'll
come another time.'

'No, no. If it is Mr Lawrence, then you are to stay,' called a
feminine voice from within, and Ekaterina appeared a few minutes
later dressed in a stunning pair of silken palazzo pants with
matching top, her blonde hair swept up in a comb from which
many artless curls descended.

She really was ravishing looking, thought Nick, turning his panama hat in his hands.

Ekaterina flashed a brilliant smile. 'Now, would you like tea or a drink, Mr Lawrence?'

He grinned awkwardly. 'Do you have any lapsang souchong?'

'Of course,' she answered. 'We stock practically everything here. And what about you, Ricardo?'

'Coke, please. Sugar free, of course.'

Obviously extremely short of servants Ekaterina went to the kitchen herself and came back with a tray clinking with glasses. She found both Nick and Ricardo standing in silence at different windows watching the two swans skimming the waters of the moat.

'They're lovely, aren't they?' she said.

'Beautiful. Were they here when you came?'

'Oh yes. I love them but Gerry wants to get rid of them and fill the moat with fish.'

'Surely you won't let him?'

'They go over my dead body,' answered Ekaterina firmly. 'He's a philistine. Come and look at what he's done to the round room.'

They followed her into the place where Gerry worked and Nick was aghast to see full-length photographs of the actor hanging alongside tapestries, precious with antiquity.

'My husband,' said Ekaterina with a non-amused laugh, 'would like to get rid of the wall hangings and paint the walls pea green.'

'You cannot be serious,' said Ricardo but Nick shook his head and added, 'But that would be sacrilege. You should add more tapestries if anything. Where did you get these by the way?'

'My father picked them up in an auction somewhere or other.'

'Was he a dealer?' Nick asked, interested.

Ekaterina grinned and said, 'Sort of.'

They returned to the tea cups and the vicar broached the reason for his visit.

'I've come to see if I can interest you in any village activities.'

She pulled a wry face. 'Frankly, I would rather go to London for my amusements. As you know I have a fast car and if I don't feel like driving I can take the train from Oakbridge. Talking of which, how is the Son et Lumière proceeding?'

Nick gave what he hoped was a gallant laugh. 'Well, your husband has one or two ideas for modernizing the show.'

'Oh dear. I'm sure they haven't gone down too well.'

'No they haven't I'm afraid.'

'Has he suggested that he does a hip-hop routine?'

'Not exactly.'

Ekaterina sighed. 'He will, you can bet on it.'

'Perhaps you could have a word with him.'

She gave an exquisite shrug. 'It would make no difference, I assure you. Gerry has always been a law unto himself.'

Ricardo spoke up. 'I'm sorry but what is this Son et Lumière you are talking about?'

Nick answered, 'It's the history of Fulke Castle, which is near here; an historic castle built in 1067. I think it is going to be awfully good.'

'That is if my husband doesn't muck it up.'

'When is it coming off?'

'In four weeks' time. Why? Are you coming to see it?'

'I would rather be in it,' Ricardo answered surprisingly.

Both Ekaterina and Nick turned on him an astonished stare.

'Well, we are still rather short of men,' the vicar ventured.

Ricardo explained. 'I am giving Mrs Harlington a course of massage and am also going to help her to find a suitable health club. So I have booked into The Great House for a month. I would very much like to find something to do in the evenings.'

'Then please come to the next rehearsal. I'm sure you would be most welcome,' said Nick.

Kasper had managed to buy himself a small but beautiful cottage in Arrow Street. It was three hundred years old, had a small garden at the back in which he could sit out, and was ideally suited to his bachelor existence. Tonight, however, he was having a small dinner party and was busy in the kitchen preparing Polish food. He had invited Nick and the owner of Fulke Castle, Sir Rufus Beaudegrave, whom he had met socially at a boring little drinks party given by Colonel and Mrs Babbs who lived in The Maze. The colonel had dressed in ginger tweeds and his wife worn a worsted plaid bias-cut skirt. The whole event had been extremely hearty and dull.

Kasper hummed as he worked and decided that this evening would be the complete opposite of dreary with plenty of vodka to drink and wild Polish dishes that he hoped the others would like. Fortunately he was a good cook and highly organized and so had a quarter of an hour to spare during which he washed and changed his shirt and wished Olivia would come back from her world tour. There could be no doubt that he liked her enormously and it would not take much persuading for him to fall totally in love. But he had competition and of that he was highly aware.

The leader of the rival faction, Nick, knocked on the front door exactly five minutes later and was seated, vodka in hand, when the knocker went again. The vicar stood up, anxious in several ways to get a look at Sir Rufus Beaudegrave, the owner of Fulke Castle.

He was a tall man, standing well over six feet, and broad of shoulder into the bargain. He had bright-red hair, rather like the smouldering remains of a log fire, strongly marked features and a very fine well-proportioned nose. His eyes were remarkable; amber pupils with tawny flecks in them. Nick thought that put a helmet and chain mail on him and he could quite easily pass for one of his ancestors.

The fourth member of the group was a girlfriend of Sir Rufus's and was vapid with a well-bred face exactly like a million others that one could see at upper-class parties. She wore her hair straight and had the habit of flicking it back with a movement of her head about every five minutes or so. She had a very short skirt on and black leggings beneath. Nick stared in fascination at her feet, which were adorned by a massive pair of red shoes with five-inch heels, a platform sole and a welter of florid red bows down the front. He had quite literally never seen anything like them. She looked down and said, 'Do you like my shoes?' in a very posh voice.

Nick gulped, not wishing to lie but conscious of the fact that to tell the truth would be hurtful. 'They're not quite what I'm used to,' he said.

'I gathered that,' she answered with a cold look and turned her head away to talk to Rufus, who was making it quite clear that she and he were just good friends.

Nick had looked Rufus Beaudegrave up on Wikipedia before he came out and had discovered that the man had been married and divorced, leaving him with the custody of four little girls. He had then looked up a copy of the *Daily Express* relevant to the divorce and learned that the wife had run off with the game-keeper and was living in a small two-bedroomed cottage in a nearby village.

What extraordinary lives some people lead, he had thought. And looking at Rufus now as they took their seats at the dinner table, he could not imagine why any woman would want to bolt from him. He supposed the answer lay in good old-fashioned sex.

Rufus was speaking. 'Have you heard about the Son et Lumière thing they are doing at my castle?'

'Yes,' said Kasper, while Nick replied, 'I'm in it actually.'

'Are you, by Jove? Then you'll have witnessed the trouble at first hand.'

The vicar decided to be honest and said, 'There isn't any real trouble, Sir Rufus.'

'That's not what I heard. In fact the local solicitor has been to see me and asked me to intercede.'

Nick looked at him blankly.

'He's in the damned thing. Name of Paul Silas. Models himself on Donald Sinden . . .'

'Oh, I know who you mean.'

'Well, he made an appointment to call on me and did nothing but grumble about the new director who is apparently a third-rate American actor who starred in the Wasp Man films.'

The girl, whose name was Davina Booth-Lyle, said, 'What can you expect with amateur dramatics? Everybody is out to put down everyone else. My sister was in a production where they cast a forty-year-old as Juliet. She turned out to be the wife of the director. How ridiculous can you get?'

'I tend to agree. But I must admit this show is going to be pretty terrific. I think it will be utterly spectacular when it is done in Fulke Castle.'

'So when is your first rehearsal in the castle?' This from Rufus.

'Tuesday night.'

'I'll come and observe.'

'I think we'd appreciate that very much.'

'Including the Wasp Man?' Rufus asked.

'Yes, if he's got any sense.'

The conversation veered away to the food, which everybody was enjoying – excepting Davina who picked at her helping with a disconsolate expression. Kasper enquired if she would rather have something else but she said no in a wispy voice. After that the men tended to ignore her.

The evening over, Rufus roared away in a large four-by-four but Nick walked up Arrow Street, quiet and deserted at this hour of the night, and back home along the High Street. As he drew alongside The Great House he stopped dead in his tracks. Even through those great Tudor walls a voice could be heard.

'Geez, you're asking me if I know Brad Pitt. Well, let me tell you sumpin. I knew Brad when he was just starting out on his career. In fact it was I myself who had a little whisper in the director's ear. Wolf, I said . . .'

Some uncouth youth let out a baying howl at this but was shushed by the others. It was obvious that Gerry had gathered quite an audience.

'Wolf, give the kid a chance. He's got the looks and I believe he's got the talent. Give him a break. I'll stake my life on the fact that he won't let you down.'

There was a kind of mock cheer, which led Nick to the conclusion that they, his audience, were collectively taking the mickey.

And what else does he deserve, thought Nick in an uncharitable way. He was beginning to think of the Wasp Man as a self-opinionated little squirt and just hoped that in some way or other he could not ruin the grand concept of the Son et Lumière.

SIX

Fulke Castle had been named after its builder, the great Norman warrior Fulke Beau de Grave, who had fought mightily at Hastings alongside his cousin Guillame, anglicized to William, the Conqueror. As a reward he had been granted great swathes of land on one of which, in 1067, he had started to build a moated motte-and-bailey castle. A stone keep was

added as the original buildings were not strong enough to with-
stand attacks from marauders and it was still possible to walk
around the immense twelfth-century walls with its ramparts
providing a magnificent view of the castle complex. During the
English Civil War it had been the only remaining Royalist strong-
hold in the south-east of England and it was besieged by
Cromwell's troops for three years before the chatelaine, Lady
Marguerite Beau de Grave, had finally conceded. To repay her
in kind, Cromwell had ordered the removal of the castle's roofs.
But the restoration of Charles II had seen the repairs undertaken
and Lady Marguerite had planted an oak tree in the courtyard to
mark the end of the castle's warlike past.

Peace had indeed returned to Fulke Castle. To the right of the
old fortifications, looking at the buildings from the drawbridge
– now replaced by an eighteenth-century bridge that could
be crossed on foot – the Tudor Beau de Graves had built a large
set of additional rooms and a great feasting room, which could
be reached by a covered passageway that spanned the moat and
contained two arches through which the water flowed peacefully.
Added on to these were the graceful Georgian buildings and
these had finally been extended by a compact Victorian dwelling,
complete with tower from which Rufus flew the Beau de Grave
flag bearing the family coat of arms. It was in this part of the
castle that he continued to live.

Nick, arriving early so that he could look round the place, felt
unbelievably excited. It was so exquisite that it made him gasp
out loud and he was glad that there was nobody around to hear
him. At the same time he felt an enormous admiration for the
family that had kept it going by a great effort of will. Rufus, so
he had been told, hired the place out for films and TV, did
weddings, ghost walks, public admittances, balloon rides, old-car
rallies, etc. He had even converted a few rooms in the Tudor
block for rich Americans to stay in luxury and be hosted to a
feast in the great dining hall. The one thing he had drawn the
line at was bed and breakfast for passing strangers. At the same
time as all this was going on he was raising four small daughters
single-handedly. Nick raised his metaphorical hat to him.

The audience for the Son et Lumière were to sit in the courtyard which had been formed by the Tudor dining hall on the

right-hand side, the Georgian buildings to the left. Immediately opposite them were the ramparts with some medieval archways underneath. Behind them stood Lady Marguerite's oak tree. Action would take place all around them, as it were, and Nick felt he must enjoin his parishioners to buy tickets as it was obviously going to be an incredible sight to witness. Feeling in good spirits he crossed the moat and made his way within.

Gerry was rushing around with a baseball cap on his head. He wore this sideways with the peak over his right ear and the back over his left. He carried a clipboard on which were attached a copy of the script and several important-looking documents. The sound people – a professional team hired from London – were quietly getting on with organizing the speakers. While the lighting people – also professional – were crawling all over the lighting rig. Meanwhile Gerry shouted instructions through a loudhailer which everybody ignored.

The actors had been given a large tent behind the scenes for costume changes and make-up and despite being early Nick discovered that a lot of the rest of the cast had done likewise. He got into his opening costume – a medieval builder – then wandered round to Marguerite's oak tree to watch what was going on. The entire acting area was now plunged into impenetrable darkness through which the only sound that could be heard was that of Gerry bellowing. And then suddenly, as if by magic, the lights began slowly to come up, bathing the old castle in an ethereal silver. It was at that moment that a white barn owl flew across the courtyard and disappeared into the darkness beyond. It was as if it had been created by supernatural means and Nick found himself transfixed. He heard the movement of someone beside him and saw that Jonquil, too, was totally enraptured.

In the dimness the sound of Rafael Devine's awe-inspiring voice spoke the opening words.

'The year is ten sixty-seven and that grim and bloody battle which would become known in history as the Battle of Hastings is over. Fighting alongside William of Normandy was his cousin and lifelong friend, Fulke Beau de Grave, present in Westminster Abbey when William, now styled the Conqueror, was crowned King of England. He was rewarded amply for his loyalty to the crown, being granted great swathes of land, one of which included a large holding in Sussex.'

The soundtrack faded out and Gerry's voice could be heard saying, 'Hey, what's going on?' only to die away as the spotlight suddenly blazed on a solitary rider coming through one of the medieval arches and looking about him in the darkness. Nick felt so inspired that he gripped the hand of the person standing next to him. He felt that he was looking on the true Fulke Beau de Grave, dressed in chain mail and flowing crimson cloak. Indeed he was so overcome with emotion that his eyes actually filled with tears.

'We'd better go round. You're on next,' a voice whispered in his ear, and he turned, much embarrassed, to see Jonquil smiling at him.

He rapidly let go of her hand, saying 'I'm sorry,' in a muffled voice.

'Don't apologize. I was feeling exactly the same as you were,' she answered.

And he could see that she really meant it.

The rest of the rehearsal went smoothly enough until it came to the show-stopper, the Elizabethan Fair scene. At this, Gerry, who had remained suspiciously quiet after his opening gaffe, called all the players into the courtyard and stood up on a chair.

'Well, kids, it's all going a gas at the moment. It's real cool. But I just thought I ought to warn you that I have slightly altered the Fair scene. I have invited a troupe of morris dancers – the Casselbury Ring Men – to perform in this scene.'

He consulted a piece of paper on his clipboard.

'As you are probably all aware, morris dancers have been around a hell of a long time. The first known reference to them was in 1448.'

He's been on the Internet, thought Nick.

'And they were very popular in Tudor times. William Kemp danced a solo morris from London to Norwich in 1600 and the Bard of Avon referred to them in one of his plays, saying, I quote, "As fit for a morris for May Day".'

There was a stunned silence.

'Anyway, these Casselbury guys are pretty busy with other

engagements and I'm afraid that they cannot be with us until the dress rehearsal, in other words the day after tomorrow. They will dance just after the gypsies have come on with the performing bear. Is that OK with everybody? 'Cos if it ain't, that's tough.'

Nick waited for somebody to raise an objection but surprisingly nobody did. Ricardo, who had joined the company ten days ago, whispered to Nick, 'Who are these people he's talking about?'

'They're quite well known. They come from West Sussex and they've named themselves after a local feature, Casselbury Ring, which is a ring of trees supposed to have mystic powers.'

'Will they spoil the show?'

'No, I don't think so. In fact they might enhance it.'

'Good.'

'OK, people,' said Gerry. 'Let's proceed.'

The actors vanished to begin the Elizabethan Fair but not before Nick had caught a glimpse of a man's face watching the proceedings from a window in the Tudor feasting hall. So Rufus had been there all the time, he thought, and Nick hoped he was impressed.

After the rehearsal was over there was the usual gathering of people in a local pub, The Beaudegrave Arms. Nick had joined them for the first time, accompanied by Ricardo, who was looking gorgeous in a silk shirt, open at the neck and displaying a beautifully waxed chest. He had obviously been spray tanned and the colour of his skin was enhanced by the mauveness of his clothes. There was quite a flutter of women wanting to sit next to him and luck had fallen on Meg Alexander, who was eyeing him up like mad.

'What do you think about the addition of morris men to the Fair?' asked Paul Silas, taking charge as always.

'I think it could work well,' answered Robin Green.

He was clad in his usual style, baggy brown shorts and sandals, with a turtleneck sweater in a slime-green shade above. Nick caught himself wondering why men with particularly nasty legs should insist on showing them and made a mental note to inspect his own carefully before next summer.

'Well I think it's just going to make the whole show too long

and unbalanced,' said Mike Alexander, determined as ever to
rock the boat. 'I mean, it was wonderful the way Ben Merryfield
wrote it and I think out of respect to his memory we should alter
nothing.'

'Rubbish,' said Annette Muffat, leaning across Meg and
addressing Ricardo directly. 'What do you think, sunshine? Let's
get your opinion.'

'I think I am too new to your show to voice such an answer,'
he answered, bestowing on her a glance fit to melt her
undergarments.

'If you ask me,' put in Estelle Yeoman, whose opinion was
much respected as she was that marvellous thing in amateur eyes,
an ex-professional, 'there's no point in belly aching about it now.
Let's wait and see what it looks like and if it's pants then we'll
go to Harlington and tell him so.'

'That sounds like a good idea to me,' said Nick mildly.

'I agree.' This from Barry Beardsley, the verruca wizard.

The plain girl called Cynthia Wensby, who could never make up
her mind, came to a decision. 'Estelle's right. We'll just have to
wait and see.'

Jonquil, who had been at the bar, slid into a small gap beside
Ricardo. 'Are you enjoying the show, both of you?'

She addressed the remark to the masseur and to Nick.

'Very much. It is so English,' Ricardo answered in his amazing
Italian accent.

Nick, remembering how he had grabbed her hand during the
opening scene, was more than somewhat effusive as he said, 'I
think it's wonderful. And the soundtrack is terrific. What a magnificent voice Rafael Devine has got. It reminds me of recordings
made by Richard Burton.'

'Absolutely right. Have you heard his *Under Milk Wood*? It's
sensational.'

'My mother saw it on the stage and raved about it.'

'My grandmother saw Burton as Henry the Fifth and stood
up and cheered,' answered Jonquil.

'What is this *Under Milk Wood*?' asked Ricardo innocently.

Nick tried to explain but realized that his efforts were wasted
as the masseur was clearly paying him no attention, preferring
to eye up Jonquil who wasn't taking any notice of him.

Estelle spoke above the general hubbub. 'Listen, folks, we've got to give a good show for the sake of young Oswald.'

Nick racked his brains and remembered an enthusiastic teenager who was hanging round on the sidelines. Gerry treated him as a general dogsbody and was forever sending the boy off to get him cups of coffee. It had been the vicar's impression that the poor child had definitely wanted to learn the craft of theatre direction and had been fobbed off rather cruelly.

He turned to Ricardo. 'How is Mrs Harlington these days? I hope she's coming to see it.'

'She is – somewhat reluctantly.'

'Why is that?'

'I think she fears that her husband is going to try and modernize the show and feels that she could not bear that. It is my belief –' Ricardo bent his handsome head and lowered his voice to a whisper – 'that they don't get on too well.'

Nick, who tried his very best not to indulge in local gossip, adopted his wise-owl look and merely said, 'Ah.'

At that precise moment Ekaterina, who was wearing a rustling creation by Vivienne Westwood, crossed her beautiful legs, and said, 'Thank you. I will have another small vodka. But remember I have to drive home.'

'We're sitting ducks for the police,' answered Sir Rufus Beaudegrave, taking her glass to refill it.

'It is just as bad in America.'

'But you're not American, surely. What is that gorgeous accent you have?'

'I was born in Russia,' she said, and offered no further information.

'I thought it was somewhere like that,' he answered.

Ekaterina looked around her. They were seated in the Victorian drawing room, elegantly furnished with comfortable sofas and deep chairs. A chaise longue rested against one wall, a large fern in a big brass pot standing beside it. The curtains were drawn against the night and Rufus had a big fire going in the generous grate.

'This is a very beautiful place,' she said appreciatively.

'This is only a quarter of it,' he answered. 'Allow me to show you round in the daylight sometime.'

'I would like that. And it is about this castle that is the indirect reason I called on you.'

'I see. Go on.'

'I believe you have a Son et Lumière taking place at the moment.'

'Yes.'

'Well, my husband has been called in to direct it.'

'Yes, Gerry Harlington. This all happened because poor Ben Merryfield died very suddenly. Anyway, what about your husband?'

Ekaterina took a sip of her drink and sat up straight. 'I do not wish to be disloyal to the poor man but frankly, my dear sir, he has very strange ideas. You see he was trained as a hip-hop dancer and he wants to modernize the show. He starred in some rather poor films about the Wasp Man. That is his background.'

Sir Rufus was suddenly all attention. 'You know, I used to enjoy those films enormously. Took my kids to see them. They couldn't get enough of them.' His expression changed. 'But I do understand what you mean. However, I watched some of the rehearsal earlier this evening and there appeared to be nothing untoward going on.'

Ekaterina emptied her glass. 'Then I am sorry to have bothered you.'

'Not at all. But you've finished your drink. Can I get you anything else?'

Ekaterina put her head on one side. 'Alas, no. As I said earlier, I must consider driving home.'

Sir Rufus put out his hand. 'I'm sorry you are going. I've really enjoyed talking to you. Please come again.'

She took it and he held her fingers a fraction longer than was necessary.

'Thank you. I will try,' she answered, and allowed him to show her out.

SEVEN

Sunday in Lakehurst. An early autumn stillness hung over the trees while the sun rose lazily through a lawn of low-lying mist. The village was unusually quiet, interrupted only by the occasional bark of a dog or the distant sound of children playing. Other than for that one could think of it as deserted or in a time warp, a Brigadoon that only appeared every hundred years. And even though on that particular morning it was only a sleepy Sussex village, it had a rich and fascinating history, much of it dark and disturbing. In recent memory there had been a series of murders perpetrated by a single hand, but years before that the village had had its share of saints and smugglers, of witches and wizardry, of deranged old men who would drive their coach and four down the cobbled road to wake up all the citizens sleeping in their dreamless couches.

As this was his busiest day of the week Nick had set his alarm for six and thus was able to witness first light, the sun huge and red as it came up through the fog. Putting on his dressing gown he paused a moment at the window, feeling a great oneness with the whole of humanity, his soul leaping and his mind questioning. But then the sensation passed and he went downstairs and fed Radetsky, who sat like a small ginger sentry at the bottom of the stairs, standing up and purring as Nick appeared.

The vicar was just conveying a spoonful of muesli to his mouth when the telephone rang. It was Gerry Harlington.

'Hi ya, Vic. How are things?'

'Well I'm going to be rather busy today. I've a couple of christenings to do this afternoon. In fact I'm not going to get any time off until this evening. I do hope you're not calling an extra rehearsal.'

Gerry laughed a trout-gurgling laugh. 'No, sir. I think the show is just fine. I've got some personal work to do on it but you needn't concern yourself with that. No, I really rang you to apologize for not coming to church today. Sorry, but the castle is calling, as they say.'

Nick felt guilty that he experienced such a terrific surge of relief at the words. 'Oh that's quite all right, Gerry. You must put your other commitments first. We want a good performance.'

'We sure do. Bye now.'

As Nick put some bread in the toaster he wondered what 'personal work' Gerry had referred to. And then he thought of the morris men – the Casselbury Ring troupe – and wondered if at last they were available and Gerry was fitting them into the show. He fervently hoped so.

Ekaterina woke early and was surprised to find that Gerry had risen before her and had gone downstairs. As she went along the dark corridor leading to the staircase she felt something brush against her arm but when she turned to see what it was there was nothing there.

'Good morning, ghost,' she said cheerfully, and proceeded downwards.

The whole of the bottom half of the house was filled by the sound of extremely loud hip-hop music, shaking the ancient timbers and making the old building shudder. With a sigh Ekaterina walked along one of the two narrow corridors that ran parallel, making her way to the old servants' quarters at the back of the building. In there Gerry had converted an ancient kitchen into a kind of gymnasium-cum-rumpus room and it was from here that the music was blaring. Ekaterina stood frozen in the doorway, watching him. He was wearing combat camouflage trousers and a black vest, the habitual baseball cap rammed down hard on his head. And he was doing an absolutely hectic hip-hop routine. At the precise moment of her arrival he was wiggling his bottom at speed and then squatting down and rising up again, only to repeat the movement two or three times. Finally he raised his arms straight above his head, revealing a great deal of armpit hair, and then lowered them, palms of hands facing the unseen audience.

'What,' said Ekaterina into the sudden silence, 'are you doing?'

Gerry jumped and answered nastily, 'What does it look as if I'm doing?'

'I have no idea.'

'I'm dancing, you silly bitch. That's what I do – hip-hop.'

'But why now?'

Gerry mopped his sweaty brow. 'Because I'm working out. I wanna keep fit. I don't belong to any fancy health club in Brighton.'

'You can join it if you want to. There's nothing stopping you.'

'Oh no? What about the money?'

Ekaterina shrugged carelessly. 'Is your allowance too small? I can increase it if that is what you would like.'

'What I would like is a joint cheque book.'

'And that is what you are not going to get. I am staying in sole control of what I inherited.'

Gerry came up close to her and thrust his face within an inch of hers. 'I think you're a parsimonious cow.'

Ekaterina stared back at him without flinching. 'Do you really?' she said icily, and started to walk away.

A big black hand approached her face and then, thinking better of it, just as quickly withdrew.

'You're trash,' said Gerry.

'Has anyone ever told you how becoming you look in those clothes,' she answered coolly and, turning on her heel, made her way back into the main part of the manor.

Inwardly she was seething, thinking that this was the final straw. She had been contemplating divorce for some months but always the thought of how much Gerry was going to make out of it had held her back. But now she felt she didn't care. He could become a millionaire. It would be cheap at the price to get rid of him. For Ekaterina had not only changed in looks but also in personality. As the beautiful swan had emerged from the knives of surgeons, based in clinics throughout the world, she had at long last realized her own worth. She had felt lovely and as a result her entire life had been altered. She no longer regarded Gerry as anything other than someone who had been kind to her when she was a squinty-eyed, frightened girl. For nowadays her suspicions that he had been checking out exactly who he was marrying had multiplied. Still cold with anger she marched upstairs and slipped on some casual clothes designed for her by Valentino. Then she made up her glorious face and left the house in her snazzy sports car.

Having nowhere in particular to drive to she found herself

making her way towards Fulke Castle, soon to be the scene of her husband's triumph. Or rather the hard work of the Odds would create the hit and he would take all the glory. Still furious, Ekaterina drove over the bridge and pulled up outside the castle.

The moat was sapphire blue in the morning sunshine and dotted with water fowl. Black swans with red beaks swam along-side those of dazzling white plumage, and ducks and moorhens were establishing their place with noisy quacks. Getting out of her car she saw that the trees were turning a fiery red after the warm summer and realized for the first time that the castle was built on a tiny island. Staring at it closely it seemed to her that the lovely location was like the domain of the Sleeping Beauty, a fairy-tale place with a magical quality all its own. Ekaterina drew breath as a mauve balloon appeared in the sky, its basket full of people drinking champagne. One of them waved at her and she waved back.

The oldest part of the castle was built out over the water and she noticed that up on the battlements of these ancient fortifica-tions a distant figure was standing, surrounded by a clutch of girls of varying sizes. Ekaterina felt sure that it was Sir Rufus and she tentatively raised an arm in greeting. To her immense pleasure the man gesticulated back and indicated that she was to stay where she was. She did so, very happy all of a sudden. It took him several minutes to reach her side but when he finally arrived she saw that he was smiling broadly.

'Hello, Mrs Harlington. I didn't expect to see you back so soon.'

'I didn't expect to be here. But I was out for a drive and my car just led me. So I allowed it to go where it wanted.'

'Does it often do that? Take you on magical mystery tours I mean.'

'Sometimes,' Ekaterina answered, and thought how fine Sir Rufus looked, his hair as red as the autumn trees, his skin fresh and clear.

'Well, now that you are here can I show you over the castle?'

'It would indeed be a great pleasure,' she answered in her careful Russian way.

'We'll start at the oldest part and then you can meet my daughters.'

'That will be nice. How long have you been looking after them?'

'Five years now. The smallest one, Perdita, was just three when her mother left me.'

'Why?' asked Ekaterina, never wasting words on niceties.

'She fell for a gamekeeper and moved into his cottage.'

'Like Lady Chatterley?'

'Just like,' Rufus answered, and they both laughed, the sound echoing off the old stones that surrounded them.

Up on the battlements his four children awaited them, going very quiet and serious as Ekaterina approached.

'This is Perdita,' Rufus announced, and the smallest came forward and said, 'Hello,' rather shyly.

'And this one is Ondine. And next to her comes Iolanthe. And my eldest girl is Araminta.'

'What beautiful names,' said Ekaterina. 'They are quite lovely – as, indeed, are their owners.'

And it was true. Only one – Iolanthe – had inherited Rufus's red hair and striking autumn looks but the rest were also truly beautiful in their own individual ways. Araminta, who presumably took after the bolting Lady Beaudegrave, had hair a-glistening, gleaming black, and was blessed with a pair of wide, jade-coloured eyes. The other two girls were both blondes but where one was tall and languid, the other was a busy little parcel, petite and doll-like. This one, Perdita, shook Ekaterina's hand and said 'Welcome to the castle.' Ekaterina, who had never felt in the least maternal, felt a strange stirring sensation in the region of her heart.

An hour later and they had seen over the entire castle, ending up in the Victorian part. As they had passed through the Tudor courtyard Ekaterina had noted the amazing lighting rig and sound equipment and could not help but remark to Rufus, 'All this is for Gerry's production, I take it?'

'You are absolutely right. I think it is going to be tremendous.'

Thinking of her husband's amazing ego and going cold at the idea, Ekaterina said, 'I hope you are correct.'

Rufus had taken her hands in his and turned to face her. 'I watched the last rehearsal and I can assure you that there was absolutely no hanky-panky.'

''Anky-panky,' she repeated in her delightful Russian accent. 'I do not know this expression. What does it mean?'

'Dubious goings-on,' replied Rufus, and his four girls tittered in harmony.

It was inevitable that he should invite her to join him for lunch, which they ate at a very ancient pub called The Brown Trout. The girls were all very well behaved but Ekaterina was well aware of the discerning gaze of Araminta, the eldest. Those jade-green eyes barely left her and she wondered if she was making a good impression. Once Ekaterina glanced up and caught Rufus looking at her with his bright amber gaze and there could be no doubt that she was creating an impact on him. Once again she had that strange feeling that somewhere inside her an icicle was melting.

By the time she returned home she was feeling guilty but happy and she walked into the moated manor house humming a little tune.

'Gerry,' she called, 'where are you?'

There was no reply but from his study she could hear the television blaring loudly. Putting her head round the door she saw him, trainers on an antique table, still wearing his smelly hip-hop clothes and fast asleep with his mouth open. Giving a deep sigh, Ekaterina withdrew to the drawing room to read *Vogue*.

After evensong Nick would gladly have slumped in front of the television but had promised Kasper that he would meet him for a pint so made his way to The Great House. Inside, Jack Boggis was relating a tale to a small man who, so legend had it, suffered extremely with poor health. And indeed the fellow was going white as a sheet as Jack held forth.

'Trouble is that the drive to Devon gave me a terrible attack of piles,' snorted Boggis, laughing and showing pale pink gums. 'As soon as I arrived I said to the woman I was going to see that my arse was killing me.'

The other fellow, who Nick believed was called Alfred Munn, asked in a ghostly whisper, 'And what did she say to that?'

'I think she was a bit annoyed because she never answered directly. But the look on her face was enough to make me die laughing.'

He took a deep quaff of ale and then guffawed so loudly that the people at the next table gave him a funny look.

Kasper rolled his eyes. 'As if we wish to know that.'

'You must hear a thing or two in your profession, though,' Nick remarked rather waggishly.

'And so must you. The secrets of the confessional and all that.'

'Quite. Anyway, when are you coming to see the Son et Lumière?'

'The first night. Is it going to be any good?'

'I saw a bit of the rehearsal the other evening and quite frankly I felt moist about the eye. With admiration, I hasten to add.'

'In that case I can't wait. I shall be in the front row.'

Nick turned to Jack. 'Excuse me interrupting your conversation, Mr Boggis, but I wondered if you would be attending the Son et Lumière that is being put on at Fulke Castle?'

'No. I don't go to local am-drams. Don't like 'em and can't pretend I do. So that's your answer, Vicar.'

'I'd like to go if I can find anyone to give me a lift,' piped up Alfred.

'I'll do that,' Kasper offered valiantly. 'I'm going on the first night.'

'Then I'll ring up for a ticket.'

Jack turned purple but said nothing. Unchristian as it was, Nick thought him a thoroughly objectionable old bore. He turned to Alfred.

'Thank you very much, Mr Munn. I'm sure you'll enjoy the show.'

'I'll pick you up at seven,' Kasper added.

'I'm looking forward to it.'

The vicar and the doctor regarded one another and neither could resist grinning.

'Round one to us,' whispered Kasper.

'Agreed,' said Nick – and they clinked glasses.

EIGHT

It was dress rehearsal night and all the cast had arrived early at the castle with the exception of Paul Silas who huffed in late saying that he had been held up at a business meeting. As ever, Gerry was rushing around with a loudhailer bellowing instructions at the lighting people who completely ignored him. They had been there all day and had been wonderfully looked after by Rufus's housekeeper who had kept them supplied with teas and coffees and rounds of sandwiches at lunchtime. Gerry had also been in conference with the sound man but this conversation had been 'sotto voce' and as all the cast were busy getting into their costumes nobody had bothered about it. Eventually Gerry had produced a stopwatch and given the order to start from his position in the back row of the audience. The sound tape had come on and Rafael Devine's wonderful voice had filled the auditorium.

Paul Silas, who had just mounted his horse, was a few seconds late making his entrance but this in no way ruined the scene which Rufus, who had just slipped into a darkened corner to watch, found as moving and heart-stirring as had Nicholas. Eventually the opening spectacle went black. Then followed the next scene – the building of the castle.

The third act was set in the year 1152 and contained the whole cast, dressed as servants and church officials and starring Sir Greville Beau de Grave – played by Mike Alexander – in trouble with the See of Canterbury. The pageant changed once more and this time to the most amazing battle scene. King John was besieging Fulke Castle. There were mounted riders everywhere and two figures fighting fiercely up on the battlements. Rufus, looking round briefly, noticed that Gerry had gone backstage. But the next second his full attention was back on the action as, with a terrible cry, a body came hurtling over the ramparts and crunched on to the ground below. He half-rose from his seat, thinking for a minute that it had been real, then relaxed as he took in that it was merely a theatrical effect, that it was a dummy that had hurtled to the ground before his eyes.

In the dressing tent Nick was gallantly squeezing into his costume for the Elizabethan Fair scene. It had obviously been made for someone much shorter and he was having trouble getting his shoulders into the suit-of-lights.

'Can I help?' asked a voice beside him, and he turned to see Jonquil Charmwood smiling attractively.

'If you could just do the buttons up at the back.'

'I'll try. Crikey, this must have been made for a midget.'

'I hope I'm not putting on weight.'

'No, you've got a good figure.' Nick felt inordinately pleased. 'It's just that the last person to wear this must have been terribly short.'

She heaved and his armpits stung with the strain as the last of the buttons were done up.

'I feel like the hunchback of Notre Dame.'

'Well, you don't look like him. What about my rig out?'

And she stepped into a bear costume and pulled the head over her face.

'An improvement,' said Nick.

Neither of them were on in the next scene in which Edward, Prince of Wales – the future Edward II – visits Fulke Castle with his favourite and lover, Piers Gaveston. The vicar had wondered if this was perhaps a little too frank in view of the children who would undoubtedly be in the audience but had been reassured by Kasper that nowadays they knew everything and he was to think no more about it.

The spectacle that followed was to be the highlight of the entire show – an Elizabethan Fair. The special features of this section were a pantomime horse and a dancing bear, lead by a busty gypsy girl – played by a member of the Odds with a frightfully strident accent but all the other necessary attributes – and her gypsy lover, the part taken by Barry Beardsley, the chiropodist, who had dark hair and looked rather dashing in the costume. Everyone was in it and there was to be dancing, pedlars selling tricks to high-born ladies and village girls, the jester cutting capers, and all rubbing shoulders with the cottars and villeins. In other words a riotous melange of music and colour. However,

so far nobody had even caught a glimpse of the promised
Casselbury Ring Men and Nick, for one, was getting worried.

'Have you seen the morris dancers?' he asked Jonquil.

The bear shook its head. 'No,' said a muffled voice.

'But they are on in the next scene.'

'I know,' came the distant reply.

'Well, where are they?'

The bear shook its head. 'I haven't a clue.'

They were silenced by Barry who said, 'Come along, dancing
beauty,' and took hold of the chain with which he was to lead
Jonquil on.

They all started to march up the slight incline towards the
castle, listening to the voice of a lyric tenor singing, 'Tricks for
my lady, to please her haughty eye upon a summer's day.' Then
came Rafael Devine's commentary. 'The year is sixteen hundred
and Elizabeth the First is on the throne of England. Come, my
people, and join the revelry of an Elizabethan Fair.'

The lights came up in full glory and Nick, doing his best,
bounded cheerfully on to the acting area, waving his jester's stick
and silently praying that his costume would not split. The recorded
music rose to full crescendo and the rest of the cast burst on to
the stage behind him.

It was indeed a feast for the eye and Rufus, still sitting in
his dark corner, smiled with enormous satisfaction to think that
his ancestors might indeed have hosted such an event. He
watched the pantomime horse capering around and felt sorry
for the dancing bear who was raising its legs in a mock jig,
while at the same time admiring the gypsy girl's bust. Then
suddenly there was a roll of drums that somehow did not seem
to fit with the rest of the tape. He waited for Rafael Devine's
commentary but there was only silence. And then, with a cry
of 'Yeah, man!' a dark figure erupted on to the scene and stood
stock still for a second, as if awaiting applause, before breaking
into a manic dance. Rufus could hardly believe his eyes.
Ekaterina's worst fears had been realized. At the very last minute
the Wasp Man had sabotaged the show.

Rufus sat transfixed, aware that he must do something but not
sure what, as Gerry – in baseball cap and camouflage gear –
gyrated like a wild thing in ecstasy, executing a hip-hop dance

for all he was worth. But if Rufus was flummoxed, it was nothing as compared to the rest of the cast. Action ground to a halt as they stood and stared in horror. It was the ex-professional actress – or actor as she would have insisted on being called – Estelle, who saved the day.

'Grand chain,' she commanded in ringing tones, and taking Paul Silas by the hand swung him round and landed in front of Nick. He stared at her momentarily before he caught on that this was a mass protest and joined in by swinging to the gypsy girl, whose enormous embonpoint hit him on the chin as they swung round each other. In this way, alternate hands being offered to those nearest, the whole company charged into action and formed a circle round the frenetic dancer until the hip-hop music finally ground to a halt.

'Stop the tape,' Gerry bellowed at the sound man.

'Yes, stop it indeed,' echoed Paul Silas menacingly.

'What the hell did you think you were doing?' the Wasp Man said loudly. 'What the hell did you mean by circling round me like that?'

'And what the hell,' asked Mike Alexander in a low and terrible voice, 'did you mean by introducing your crappy dance into an Elizabethan Fair scene? Have you no sense of history, man?'

'Sure I have,' Gerry answered nonchalantly. 'It was just that I thought your show could do with a bit of modernizing. I said that right from the start.'

'But nobody agreed with you.'

'Well, you should have made your point clearer at the time,' Gerry said, and half turned away.

There was an eruption in the crowd and Robin Green, dressed in baggy leggings and ill-fitting hose which could almost, at a distance, be taken for his usual brown shorts, rushed at Gerry and seized him by the neck. People gaped; the man was hysterical.

'You bastard,' he shouted, closing his grip on the Wasp Man's throat, 'how could you? How dare you interfere with that lovely script and beautiful concept of Ben Merryfield's? I could strangle you. You beastly rat.'

And he proceeded to do just that to the accompaniment of a loud shriek from Ivy Bagshot, who fainted in a heap at the feet of the bear. Jonquil whipped off the bear's head and shouted at Nick, 'Do something, for God's sake. He really will do it, you know.'

The vicar leapt forward in the company of Barry Beardsley who was manfully attempting to drag Robin off the Wasp Man. Paul Silas, meanwhile, had added his heavyweight skills in what appeared to be a judo hold on Mr Green's lower ends. Nick, wondering if he was going to be any use at all, jumped headlong on the whole fighting crew and brought them crashing to the ground. Gerry got to his feet panting and poor spotty Oswald, the teenager who had joined the show in a desperate attempt to learn the skills of directing, hurried to his side.

'Can I get you a glass of water, Mr Harlington?'

'Get me a glass of vodka, more like. And pick up my cap for me.'

The baseball headgear had fallen to the ground in the melee and Oswald, retrieving it, handed it to Gerry who rammed it firmly on his head.

'I resign from your shitty show,' he said. 'I quit. I should never have joined you bunch of amateurs in the first place.'

Paul Silas said, 'I think we can manage perfectly well, thank you.'

'Aw, fuck the lot of you,' answered Gerry and marched off in the direction of the hill.

There was a grim silence into which Oswald spoke in a whisper. 'Can we really manage without him?'

'Of course we can,' answered the large blonde Annette.

'Don't you be so sure,' came a distant voice. 'Nobody gets the better of the Wasp Man.'

To Nick, who found he had split the jester's costume down the sides during the tussle, the words had a sinister ring. And, looking round, he discovered that he was not the only one thinking so.

Barry Beardsley gave a shiver and said, 'I hope that doesn't mean he's planning some awful sort of revenge.'

'Of course it doesn't,' answered Estelle briskly. 'The man's all mouth and no trousers. I suggest that we continue with the dress rehearsal. Everyone in agreement?'

There was a half-hearted answer of 'yes' and she turned to the sound man. 'Would you mind deleting that last bit of tape?'

'You mean you want it restored to the original?'

'Yes, please. Now then everybody, let's go on from where we were so arrogantly interrupted.'

The very way that Gerry drove his car up the driveway leading to the moat sent alarm bells ringing in Ekaterina's brain. Glancing at her watch she saw that he was back from the dress rehearsal extremely early and knew at once that something had gone terribly wrong. Having no wish to face her husband in this darkest of moods, she attempted a tactical withdrawal up the stairs. But from the hallway he shouted after her.

'Come here, you bitch.'

'No,' Ekaterina answered haughtily.

He ran up the stairs two at a time and caught up with her as she hurried towards the bedroom.

'When I say wait, I mean it. Understand?'

He caught her arm in a truly painful grip.

'Gerry, let go of me. You're hurting.'

'Good. It's your fault that I have to associate with that crew of amateur shit. If we lived like other couples do, with a joint cheque book, I would have my own studios in Hollywood by now. You've ruined my life, you evil grabbing cow.'

'But it's my money, Gerry.'

For an answer he slapped her on the mouth so hard that she feared she might have lost a tooth. Then he turned on his heel and went downstairs to his rumpus room. Ekaterina ran into her bedroom where she picked up the telephone.

Much to her surprise Rufus answered straight away. 'Beaudegrave.'

'Excuse me, Sir Rufus, for ringing you but Gerry has just entered the house in the fiercest of tempers. Did something go wrong at the dress rehearsal?'

'I'll say it did.' And he proceeded to tell her that she had been quite right, that Gerry had interposed a hip-hop dance into the Elizabethan Fair scene.

Ekaterina froze, imagining the full horror of what she was being told. 'What did you do?' she breathed eventually.

'Nothing. The Odds were already having a go. One of them nearly strangled him. The last I saw of your husband was stalking off towards his car with that tragic boy Oswald running after him. Ekaterina was strangely quiet and Rufus added, 'Don't be too upset about it. I'm sure it's all been sorted out.'

Ekaterina made a strange gulping sound and Rufus realized that she was weeping.

'Please, don't disturb yourself, Mrs Harlington. It was nothing to do with you.'

'Please don't call me by that name any more, Sir Rufus. I am definitely divorcing my husband. This is the straw that breaks the camel's back. I am called Ekaterina and I beg you to use that from now on.'

Her Russian accent was becoming more pronounced and Rufus could not help but smile. The fact was that she intrigued him.

'Listen,' he said, 'why not come round to the castle tomorrow evening and we can watch the show from the Tudor dining hall.'

'Yes,' she answered without hesitation. 'I would like that very much.'

'Good. I'll expect you at about six. By the way, my youngest daughter has decided you are a Russian princess.'

She laughed a little weakly. 'Tell her thank you. See you tomorrow then.'

'Yes. Goodbye.'

He hung up and wondered why he had an odd sensation of foreboding.

NINE

Kasper's last patient was suffering with an acute case of hypochondria and visited him virtually every week. But tonight he really could have done without her.

'But Dr Rudniski I have such a sniffy cold and I am suffering terribly with a pain in my heart that seems to be there all the time. What shall I do?'

He gave her a charming smile, then said, 'I'm afraid I cannot help you with the cold. Just take lots of vitamin C and inhale if it should pass on to your chest. As for your heart, I shall write to Pemley Hospital and ask one of their consultants to see you.'

'But aren't you going to listen to it?'

With a sigh Kasper reached for his stethoscope and went through the weekly routine of listening to Mrs Mimms's healthy and regular beat.

Madisson, the beautician, was also hurrying through a late appointment and had one eye on the clock as she bade her last customer farewell and hurriedly locked up the shop, putting the day's takings in a hidden safe. She barely had time to give herself a quick glance and reassure herself that she was as blonde and thin as ever, before changing into ridiculously high heels and teetering off to her car. She had a ticket for the first night of the Son et Lumière and didn't want to miss a minute of it, partly because a divinely handsome masseur called Ricardo, who had eyed her up in The Great House, was taking part in it.

Madisson was almost the last person in Fulke Castle's car park and was wobbling over the bridge when she heard hasty footsteps behind her and, turning, saw the doctor accompanied by an old fellow called Alfred Munn.

'Good evening, Dr Rudniski. I think I'm terribly late.'

'So am I. Let me help you.'

Before she could refuse he had taken her by the arm and propelled her inwards at some speed, high heels clacking like mad on the cobbles. Fortunately there were still one or two people making their way to their seats and Kasper found his place in the front row, with Madisson, by a strange coincidence, seated directly behind him. Alfred was some way back. They all sat down, a bit out of breath, and then the lights went out and they were plunged into total blackness, into the silence of which Rafael Devine spoke the opening words of the show.

Kasper, who had a great knowledge of Polish history but a rather sketchy idea of English, was transported. From the moment that Fulke Beau de Grave rode gallantly into the floodlights he was totally absorbed by the whole story. He watched the building of the castle, recognizing Nick in humble leggings and tunic, laying bricks with the best of them. Then his eyes widened at the following enactment of Sir Greville Beau de Grave's falling out with the See of Canterbury. The costumes were particularly good, he thought, particularly those of the high churchmen. The lights went out again and this time he heard the unmistakable thudding of horses' hooves in the darkness. His blood quickened as the scene of the besieging by King John was revealed and suddenly there were mounted, fighting men literally all over the castle. But his gaze was drawn up to the battlements where two knights dressed in chain mail and helmets were slugging it out for grim death.

Kasper had never seen such a realistic battle and behind him he heard Madisson squeal with excitement. The two fighters were going at it as if their very lives depended on the outcome, then suddenly one of them unexpectedly fell backwards, hitting the floor, and a second or so later a ghastly scream rang out and the one left standing heaved over the parapet, his body crunching on to the ground below. There was a shocked silence then a stir in the audience and Kasper half rose out of his seat until someone near him said, 'It's only a dummy,' and he relaxed back again. He felt Madisson tap his shoulder and turned his head.

'It *was* a dummy wasn't it?'

'Yes, of course. But I must say it was extremely realistic.'

'Scared me stiff.'

The show continued, getting more luscious with every scene that passed. Edward, Prince of Wales and Piers Gaveston dripped honey all over one another, then came the lovely spectacle of the Elizabethan Fair. Madisson could be heard shrieking with laughter at the antics of the pantomime horse and giving a discreet whistle at a gorgeous-looking young man who was playing the part of a pedlar, from whom everybody seemed to be buying something.

Up in the Tudor banqueting room Ekaterina exclaimed to Sir Rufus, 'Goodness, that is my masseur. He's staying in Lakehurst. I'm glad he joined the show.'

Araminta, who was sitting close to Ekaterina and who obviously admired her enormously, said, 'Do you have a masseur just for you?'

Ekaterina looked casual. 'He comes to my house most days. I think he is between jobs.'

'He's very good-looking.'

'Don't tell him. I believe he is rather in love with himself.'

Rufus said nothing but poured Ekaterina another glass of wine. She looked at him and thought that she could spend the rest of her life like this.

'Was it at this point that Gerry made a scene?' she asked, as the Elizabethan Fair reached a splendid climax with the jester escorting forward the Queen herself.

'Yes. But thankfully there's no sign of him tonight.'

'The Odds must have frightened him off. Although . . .' Ekaterina added thoughtfully, 'he is not the type to be easily scared.'

'Yes, but one of them was actually trying to strangle him. It was an absolute melee. I was thinking of joining in myself but they suddenly toppled over and Gerry got free. What sort of a mood has he been in today?'

'I haven't seen him. He slept in a guest room last night and was off at the crack of dawn.'

'Perhaps he's up to something.'

'Perhaps. But at least he hasn't spoiled the show.'

'No, thank God.'

The Elizabethan scene ended to much applause and yet again the audience was plunged into blackness. When the lights went up it was to reveal a troop of Roundheads coming to arrest Sir Giles Beau de Grave for his support of Charles I. A tremendous skirmish was fought with Nick manfully throwing anything he could lay his hands on at the soldiers before further reinforcements arrived. Rafael Devine's voice soared over the ensuing chaos.

'The Lady Marguerite Beau de Grave held the castle for three years after her husband was smuggled out dressed as a woman.'

Paul Silas, in drag, minced past a group of the militia who called out rude remarks as she passed.

'But then she was finally forced to surrender and Cromwell, to repay her in kind, ordered that every roof in Fulke Castle should be removed. Thus it stood, empty and ruinous, until the restoration of Charles II, who personally saw to it that all the repairs were undertaken.'

The lights dimmed and a single spotlight came up into which stepped Ivy Bagshot looking, Kasper thought, quite tall and graceful.

'To mark the end of Fulke Castle's war-torn years, Lady Marguerite planted an oak tree in the courtyard, which grows and flourishes to this day. It was to symbolize an age of peace and harmony that came to the castle at last, putting an end to its violent and bloody history.'

The lights subtly changed adding a warm glow to the surroundings and the next scene appeared, taking place in the year 1790 when Georgian buildings were added to the castle. Mr Hooker, a Georgian architect, walked round with Sir Rollo Beaudegrave, together with his wife and innumerable children, looking at the plans and talking about how he foresaw the buildings works proceeding.

Then came the familiar darkness and once more Rafael Devine's glorious voice brought the magnificent show to its end.

'In 1918, with the Victorian part of Fulke Castle built and the family settled therein, nothing could have pleased Sir Edward Beaudegrave and his wife Violet more than when their son returned triumphant at the end of the Great War. Captain Rupert had fought bravely alongside his men and had been awarded with a Military Cross . . .'

'My great-grandfather,' Rufus whispered with pride to Ekaterina.

'. . . for his efforts. Soon the house became full of young people celebrating the twenties in style and Captain Rupert was one of them.'

The warm lights came up with every member of the cast on stage. Barry Beardsley (as the Captain) was doing an energetic Charleston with Estelle Yeoman, in the midst of a crowd of others all dancing to the best of their ability. Kasper spotted Nick in evening gear doing his best to keep up with the rest of the company. He also couldn't help but notice the Italian Stallion dancing like a professional and looking somewhat like Rudolf Valentino with his black hair slicked back tightly.

'So there our story ends. The future of Fulke Castle is assured. It still stands, beautiful and proud, dominating its moat. It has dealt with war and suffering, peace and plenty, and now has become a magnificent tribute to a great and glorious past.'

At these words someone touched a switch and the entire castle was floodlit, its image brilliantly reflected in the water beneath.

The effect was both breathtaking and somehow shocking but it had the desired effect upon the audience who rose to their feet and cheered both loud and long. In the Tudor dining hall Ekaterina burst into tears and threw herself into Araminta's arms.

'Oh it was wonderful, wonderful,' she kept repeating, until Rufus took over from his daughter and administered a large and very white handkerchief.

Below, in the courtyard, Kasper was wildly excited and so was Madisson, who was whistling and shouting like a mad thing. However, the company did not take a bow, the ending being so dramatic and magical that it had been generally decided that to do so would ruin the illusion.

There had only been one snag backstage and that had been when the burly stagehand – Charlie Higgs – whose job it was to clear the dummy from the set after its dramatic fall from the battlements, had found it hard to pick up. In the pitch darkness he had decided that somebody had stuffed stones inside it for a joke and had murmured, 'Very funny!' as he had heaved it away under one of the arches. There it would be left until tomorrow night when it would be picked up and carried to the battlements before the show began.

So it was that the dummy lay alone all that long night, its eyes gazing up at the stars until eventually they faded and dawn slowly lit the beautiful building of Fulke Castle, turning it the colour of a rose. Then the dummy gave a long harsh sigh and slowly lowered its broken eyelids in the last and final sleep of all.

TEN

Like a charging herd of elephants the cast, as one, headed for The Beaudegrave Arms as soon as they had changed out of their costumes. They had arranged with the landlord to get a large round ready and they rushed for their tray standing at the corner of the bar and pounced on their glasses, which they raised in a toast.

'Here's to the show,' said Paul Silas, and proceeded to pour a pint of beer down his throat without pausing.

'The show,' repeated the others, and clinked glasses happily.

Paul completed his enormous swallow and said, 'Damn shame about Adam Gillow not turning up. Where the hell was the man?'

Robin Green, back in his shorts and sandals, put down his gin and tonic. 'What do you mean he didn't turn up? I fought with him on the battlements tonight. He was here all right.'

'Well, where did he get to for the rest of the show? He wasn't in any of the other scenes. Was he?'

Paul turned to the rest of the cast who were variously drinking and enjoying.

'Well, he definitely wasn't at the end because I had to do the Charleston on my own,' said plain-faced Cynthia Wensby plaintively.

'I didn't see him in the Elizabethan Fair,' remarked Nick, putting in his twopenn'orth.

'Well I don't care whether you saw him or not,' answered Robin. 'He fought me on the battlements until someone hit me in the legs and I fell over, and that's that.'

'Perhaps you wounded him mortally,' said Ricardo, and everybody laughed.

It had been a happy team, Nick considered, though he had to admit that the scene at the dress rehearsal had been very unpleasant. He, along with many other members of the cast, had wondered whether Gerry Harlington was plotting some terrible revenge for tonight but they had come through this evening not only unscathed but in triumph. Of Mr Harlington there had been no sign. All was apparently well.

'Must you really go home?' said Rufus Beaudegrave. 'We have a million guest rooms if you would like to stay.'

'Don't exaggerate, Daddy. We've only got about thirty,' Araminta answered, clutching on to Ekaterina's arm.

'No, I really must get back. Thank you very much all the same. Another day I would like to come, that is if I may?'

'You're welcome here any time. Now girls, say goodnight. I'm just going to walk Ekaterina back to her car.'

Rufus's daughters automatically lined up according to height looking a little like something from *The Sound of Music*.

Ekaterina laughed delightedly. 'Do you always do that?'

'Oh yes. It was something grandma taught us,' said Araminta.

'Well, you must tell her that it looks good. She still lives, yes?'

'Indeed she does. My mother is very much alive and is more like Maggie Smith in a character role than Maggie Smith, if you see what I mean.'

'Perhaps one day I will meet her.'

'Yes, perhaps you will.'

They walked in an easy silence to Ekaterina's car, then she turned to Rufus and very simply held out her hand. He took it and kissed it, held it a moment longer than was necessary, then said, 'Come again,' and walked away. With a sigh she got into the driving seat and drove off into the darkness.

Nick had spent the early part of the night sleeping like a log, having thoroughly enjoyed his first venture into amateur drama since he had left university. But round about dawn he woke with a start and wondered if his resident ghost, William, had banged something. Yet all was quiet. Nonetheless, Nick rose, slipped on a dressing gown and went downstairs. Hearing someone in the house, Radetsky, the cat, zoomed through the cat flap and stropped round Nick's ankles.

'It's too early for breakfast. You'll have to eat your biscuits,' Nick said.

The cat gave him a knowing look from vivid emerald eyes and obligingly started to munch his way through a bowl of Catkins Poultry and Vegetables Tucker. Nick put the kettle on and made himself a cup of lapsang souchong. Then he sat in the living room and wondered what it was that could possibly be worrying him.

The congregation at the church was steadily growing. Only by one every other month, but these were regulars who smiled at him on the way out and shook his hand. He had found a cleaner and a gardener so as far as those chores were concerned he was well catered for. He was missing Olvia Beauchamp but had to admit to himself that he was very interested in Jonquil Charmwood, who was turning out to be as pleasing a personality as she was easy on the eye. Nothing wrong in that area. And then he hit on it. The fight at the dress rehearsal when Robin Green had leapt on Gerry Harlington, a mass of snarling sinew with skinny brown legs, and had started to strangle the life out of him, had been very upsetting to say the least. And what had happened to Gerry meanwhile? If the vicar had read the black man's character correctly he would never allow a slur to his manhood to go unpunished like that. On the contrary, he would have made it his personal business to seek revenge. So where was he?

Nick sipped his tea and thought that when a decent hour had been reached he would phone Gerry and ask how he was, for surely he must have gone home by now. Knowing that he was wide awake and further sleep was impossible Nick had a shower and prepared for the day ahead.

Paul Silas woke at seven o'clock and stared at the sleeping figure of his wife, thinking to himself that she was not ageing well. Little puffs of fat had gathered at her chin and her mouth was puckered, surrounded by small sharp lines. Her hair, dyed middle-aged blonde, hung shoulder length and was dead straight, emulating the style of girls thirty years younger who all, in Paul's opinion, looked as if they had been hauled up from the bowels of a river and left to drain out. Heaving a sigh he got out of bed and looked at himself in a full-length mirror.

He was still in good shape, there could be no doubt about that. Pulling his stomach in and holding his breath he looked like a man of thirty – or thereabouts. Fit enough nonetheless to play the Scarlet Pimpernel, which was one of the titles that the Odds were considering for their next production. Naturally Mike and Meg Alexander wanted to do a two-hander, *Heloise and Abelard*, but Paul had informed them in no uncertain terms that they must hire a hall and put it on privately if they wished to continue down that route.

Stark naked, he walked to the kitchen and boiled the kettle to make some coffee in the cafetière and while he waited played back the answerphone messages from last night. There were two that hung up rather than speak to a machine, a third call for Elspeth, then came the fourth – and Paul shivered as he heard it.

'Oh hello, this is a message for Paul Silas. It's from Eileen Gillow, Adam's wife. Adam is terribly sorry but he won't be able to make the performance tonight. There's been an accident at Waterloo station and all the trains are being diverted via Redhill. He's phoned to say he won't be back till ten at the earliest and to make his apologies. Sorry for any inconvenience.'

Paul could hardly believe his ears and he sank back in a chair as the full import of the words bore in on him. Somebody had fought Robin Green up on the battlements but that somebody had not been Adam Gillow. So who the hell was it? And without waiting for anything further to happen, Paul picked up the phone and dialled a number.

Ekaterina woke at dawn and gazed up at her ceiling, which was tinted pink with little ripples from the moat reflected on it. Just for a minute she lay thus, thinking about how good the show had been last night and how much she liked Rufus and how she, who had never particularly wanted children, had felt the stirring of an unknown feeling when she was in the company of his four well-behaved daughters. And then anxiety struck her as she suddenly realized that for the second night running Gerry had not appeared in the bedroom and, indeed, she had not set eyes on him for nearly forty-eight hours. Getting out of bed and pulling on her dressing gown she ran down the corridor calling his name.

Opening the door of every guest room she peered within but they were all empty, the beds undisturbed. Now she was starting to panic and rushed down the stairs and straight to the big room at the back where he had a gym plus sound equipment. The stillness frightened her. There was nobody around and the very air of the house told her that he had not been inside it for hours. She looked at the kitchen clock and saw that it was only a quarter to seven. Perhaps he had finally walked out on her, given up on their farce of a marriage. Yet she held the purse strings – in fact she was the sole source of Gerry's income – so she doubted very much that he would sacrifice such a lucrative situation. And yet, of course, if he were to divorce her he would be entitled to half her estate and that would be worth a fortune. Suddenly Ekaterina didn't care any more. She was sick of him. As far as she was concerned he could have the money and was welcome to it. The ugly duckling he had married had turned into the queen of the swans and from now on he could go his own way. Ekaterina had mentally swatted the Wasp Man and she laughed to herself at the thought.

Rufus Beaudegrave had hardly slept, full of excitement at the splendour of the Son et Lumière and the reception of the audience. The Odds might well be a mismatched bunch of amateurs but they had come together and delivered excellent performances in this particular show. And it had been made all the more wonderful by Ekaterina – that lovely, warm and tremendously beautiful Russian woman – bursting into tears of joy at the end. He pulled himself up, remembering that she was married to that American actor, the one who had ruined the show at the dress rehearsal of the Elizabethan Fair by executing the most ghastly dance he had ever seen. Rufus admitted to himself that he had smiled broadly when Gerry had been leapt on by the funny little man who always wore shorts. It was only when he had seen that the chap was strangling the life out of the creep that he had made a move to stop it. But too late. The struggling couple had vanished in a pile of arms and legs and that had been the end of that. But how that lovely girl had ever become entangled with the Wasp Man Rufus had no idea.

As dawn had crept over the moat and lit the castle with its early-morning pallor Rufus got out of his four-poster bed – which had been in the family for two hundred years though now with a thoroughly modern mattress – and put on jeans and a sweater. Going to the kitchen he made himself a swift cup of coffee and whistled to the old spaniel that lay patiently in its basket, regarding him with a mournful brown eye. Then the two of them set forth for a morning walk round the island on which the castle was built. Going round the Victorian addition first, Rufus slowly made his way towards the setting of last night's Son et Lumière and felt a swell of pride at his tremendous ancestry. Mind you, with the castle entailed as it was, it would all pass to his wastrel of a brother when he died. But there you are, there was nothing he could do about it. Unless, of course, he were to remarry and produce a son. Rufus drew in a breath hard. He was daydreaming and it would do neither him nor anybody else any good.

He had arrived under the ancient battlements where the mock fight had taken place last night and was just about to move away when his dog, old Moses, suddenly started to whine then began to sniff and paw at something lying there.

'Come on, Moses,' shouted Rufus. 'Leave it, whatever it is.'

But the dog persisted and in the end his owner crossed over to see what it was that was so interesting.

It was the dummy that had crashed so convincingly on to the cobbles below. But something about it was so strangely lifelike that Rufus paused for a moment and nudged it with his foot. The helmet shifted slightly and Rufus's attention was riveted. Instead of the stitched up man of straw that he had expected to see he could glimpse a human eyelid, closed. Suddenly he was shaking all over as he knelt down and gingerly removed the helmet, which he had to struggle to take off. Inside, a smashed skull covered with a congealing mess of sticky blood lay together with what was left of a black man's face. The Wasp Man had danced for the very last time.

ELEVEN

Inspector Dominic Tennant was having an easy morning. Last night he had appeared on Meridian News talking about a homophobic assault that had ended with the victim dying of multiple stab wounds in an alleyway in Brighton. Fortunately there had been a number of witnesses, one of whom had been able to give the police names. There had been subsequent arrests and the perpetrators had been charged. As far as he was concerned the case was closed.

He had stood by a police car for the interview, wearing his long coat, his curly hair accentuated by the street lamps, and had spoken clearly and directly to the girl from Meridian.

'Can you tell us, Inspector, whether this murder was racially motivated?'

'No, it was a gang of gay bashers –' Tennant had paused and put it into polite English – 'homophobes – who are said to have caused Mr Kazir's death. The fact that he was of Asian origin was coincidental.'

'And they are now in prison?'

'Yes. They will be tried at Lewes Assizes later this year.'

'Thank you, Inspector.'

The Meridian interviewer had insisted on him taking her card and had smiled at him quite saucily. In return, Tennant had presented his card with a flourish and had then got into a car and been driven home. And now he was having a relaxing morning pottering about his new flat.

It was situated on the top floor of a Victorian mansion, built in the quiet part of Lewes, away from the one-way system and in an area that had once been genteel and in a way still was. Professional people lived nearby and the children who played outside were controllable and polite. Tennant liked it very much and had taken considerable pleasure in furnishing it to his taste. The walls of his living room were a rich, riotous red and curtains in a matching shade hung to the floor. After that his money had become somewhat stretched and he was doing the rest of the work at his leisure, or rather when he felt in funds.

He was standing in the rather tired-looking roof garden, which had been started by the previous owner, thinking he must definitely put some work into it before the spring when the telephone rang. Somehow the very sound of the bell had a slightly menacing tone. Reluctantly Tennant picked up the receiver and said his name.

'Hello, sir, sorry to bother you but something rather important's come up.' It was Potter.

Tennant groaned silently. 'I was meant to be having a day off.'

'I know, sir. But I think you're going to like this one.'

'Tell me.'

'The body of an actor has been found at Fulke Castle . . .'

'That's not far from Lakehurst, isn't it?'

'About eight miles away. Anyway, we've had a call from Sir Rufus Beaudegrave, the owner. He sounded extremely shaken. Apparently he and his dog found the body on an early morning walk. The dead man was Gerry Harlington, who played the part of the Wasp Man in films. He was also a hip-hop dancer.'

'Good God! What part did you say he took?'

'The Wasp Man. I saw *The Revenge of the Wasp Man* a couple of years ago. It was pretty terrible but my nephews enjoyed it.'

'I'll come in.'

Fifteen minutes later Tennant walked into the sprawling police headquarters in Lewes and as luck would have it bumped into Superintendent Miller on the stairs.

'Ah, Dominic, good man. Come to my office in five minutes will you.'

'Yes, sir. Anything in particular?'

'Indeed. It's about the death at Fulke Castle. I've had Sir Rufus Beaudegrave on the phone and he feels very concerned about the whole thing. Fact is, I've met him socially on a couple of occasions and I rather liked the fellow. Anyway, we'll discuss the whole thing in depth in a few minutes.'

It was obvious that the boss man was heading for the loo and Tennant stood to one side to let him pass, then made his way to his sergeant's desk. Potter was not there but Tennant tracked him down at the coffee machine.

'Get one for me, will you.'

Potter, as neat and as orderly as ever, duly pressed the button for a black coffee without sugar and waited while the liquid poured into a plastic cup.

'There you are, sir.'

'I think we're on the Fulke Castle case,' said Tennant, sipping the rather unpleasant brew.

'I hope we are,' Potter answered enthusiastically.

'Why? Are you a fan of the hip-hop dancer?'

His sergeant pulled a face. 'No. It's just that I like the castle. I went on a tour there once and I thought it was wonderful. It's fully moated, you know.'

'How do they get on and off then?'

'Oh, they've built a causeway. Did you see the remake of *Ivanhoe* on television last year?'

'Yes. Was that Fulke Castle?'

'It certainly was, sir. Apparently the owner, Sir Rufus Beaudegrave, manages to keep the place running by letting it out for God knows what. It's been in his family since the Conquest and he's determined to keep it that way.'

'An enterprising fellow.'

'Very much so, I believe.'

At that moment they were called into Superintendent Miller's office and half an hour later were driving out into deepest Sussex. The local policeman had been called in and was standing by the body, which had been left exactly as it was, protected by the usual police tape which had been stretched across the archways surrounding it. Tennant and Potter, approaching, looked down silently on the upturned face of Gerry Harlington, the knight's helmet that had hidden it still lying where Rufus had placed it. Sir Rufus himself was standing just outside the tape, talking to another policeman who was treating him as if he were royalty. Tennant approached.

'Good afternoon, sir. I'm Dominic Tennant of the Sussex police and this is my sergeant, Mark Potter.'

'How do you do,' said Rufus politely.

'I believe it was you that found the body, Sir Rufus. Can you tell me more about that please?'

'Certainly. I knew the victim vaguely. His name was Gerry Harlington and he was a small-time actor in Hollywood. He also . . .'

Tennant interrupted tactfully. 'I have had a run down on the man's career already but if you could help me with any new information I'd be awfully grateful.'

'Such as?' Rufus enquired.

'I believe he and his wife moved to Lakehurst recently, buying the moated manor house out at Speckled Wood. And then he volunteered to direct some play or other for the Oakbridge Dramatists and Dramatic Society, which was to be performed here at the castle. Could you tell me about that.'

'It was not a play, it was a Son et Lumière, and it was the history of the castle being re-enacted in scenes. It was written by a professional writer – Bob Merryfield, he used to work at the BBC – and I must say it was a profoundly colourful and moving show. But unfortunately Bob died during rehearsals and that's when Gerry Harlington stepped in.'

'He wasn't popular?'

Rufus's colour suddenly came up and Potter shot his boss a look of surprise.

'He tried to ruin the whole thing. First of all he wanted to turn it into a musical – songs written by himself, of course. When the Odds objected he decided to introduce a hip-hop dance into the Elizabethan Fair scene. And he actually did one at the dress rehearsal. That's when the proverbial hit the fan, I can tell you.'

Tennant looked at Potter who was scribbling like mad in his notebook.

'What happened?' Tennant asked.

'He was physically attacked. Robin Green actually leapt on him and there was a terrible melee.' A smile briefly lit Rufus's face. 'Even the vicar was involved.'

The inspector looked up intently. 'Which vicar would that be?'

'The one at Lakehurst. Nice chap. Name of Lawrence.'

Tennant and Potter exchanged a grin.

'Oh yes. We've come across him before. But please continue.'

'Well, the fight was stopped and Harlington sloped off swearing revenge. And that was it really. Nothing further was seen of him. But somehow or other he must have taken the place of the man who does the stage fight with Robin Green and then – God knows how – fallen over the parapet and got himself killed.'

'So you think it was an accident?'

'Well, what else could it be?'

'I'll keep an open mind on that until we have the pathologist's report. But tell me, why did no one notice that anything was amiss during the actual show?'

'Because the fight scene was carefully rehearsed and everyone was aware it was going on. As I said, Robin Green and Adam Gillow fought up there –' he pointed to the battlements above, starkly outlined against the autumnal afternoon sky – 'and at a certain point Adam ducked down and then threw a dummy off the battlements. And most effective it was too.'

'I see. Anything else?'

'There was one funny thing, now you ask.'

'What was that?'

'Robin tripped and lost his footing. Fell over backwards in other words.'

'And that hadn't been rehearsed?'

'Definitely not. It was a complete accident.'

'And then what happened?'

'The dummy was thrown over and the lights went out. End of scene.'

'And the dummy? Where did that live?'

'That was taken up to the battlements before the show began. It was lying there all the time.'

'Most interesting.'

Tennant turned round at the sound of noises behind him and saw the familiar sight of white-clad masked figures making their way over the causeway. In their midst was the doctor – a tall, auburn-haired fresh-faced Cornish girl with whom Tennant had worked once before. She knelt down beside the body and began her examination.

Tennant turned back to Sir Rufus. 'Can you give me any idea of the whereabouts of Mrs Harlington? That is, if you know?'

'I should imagine that she is at home, Inspector. I really couldn't tell you.'

Did he mistake it or was the baronet now extremely pink in the cheeks? A becoming look with his red hair and tall build.

'Well, thank you so much for your time, Sir Rufus. I'm afraid there will be some further questions but that will be all for the moment.'

Tennant and Potter turned away and crossed over the bridged causeway on foot, making their way towards the gatehouse and beyond where a police van had been parked. There they changed into their blue protective suiting ready to inspect the body at close range. The remains of Gerry Harlington, having been photographed from all angles, had now been stripped of its chain mail and was down to the garments worn beneath. These consisted of a bloodstained T-shirt bearing the slogan 'Wasp Man For Ever – Yay' and a pair of black tights. The doctor was on the point of raising the shirt to look at the wounds beneath.

'Is this a terrible accident do you think?' Tennant asked the Cornish girl whose name was Helena Wensby.

'Could be. But I don't quite see how he could have toppled over.'

'Unless he tripped and lost his balance. But then surely the other fellow – what was his name, Potter?'

'Robin Green, sir.'

'Green, would have raised the alarm, performance or no performance.'

'Unless he didn't see,' said Helena.

'Oh come on, this is getting more and more unlikely.'

'I quite agree,' Potter answered.

The chest was covered with lacerations, mostly caused by the fall, but it was the skull that was the most terrible sight. Harlington must have landed head first, for the brains were visible and the cranium had been split in two. There were bruises to his cheeks and there were little rivulets in the dust marks caused by the helmet. Tennant leaned extremely close and the smell of drying blood filled his nostrils, making him silently heave.

'Look at this, Potter,' he called, pointing to Gerry's eyes.

The sergeant bent low. 'What is it, sir?'

'It looks to me as if Gerry was crying. I'll ask the forensics team to take a sample.'

'Good idea,' Helena answered cheerily. She stared at Tennant. 'How can he have cried?'

'Perhaps it took him a while to die,' the inspector answered sombrely, and, straightening up, turned to look at the moat.

A few minutes later, Tennant and Potter climbed up to the battlements to see the place where the stage fight had taken place. The sergeant, who had absolutely no head for heights, was looking somewhat grey about the gills but Tennant, stepping through the door at the top of the spiral staircase, exclaimed, 'My God, what a place. D'you know I envy Rufus Beaudegrave. I would like to have inherited this little lot.'

Potter gasped and held on to the battlement wall, not daring to gaze round. Tennant meanwhile was breathing in and out noisily.

'What a view. Glorious, isn't it. Good Lord, there are black swans on the moat. Take a look, Potter.'

'No thank you, sir. I'll just stay where I am if it's all the same to you.'

Tennant glanced over. 'Oh dear. It is a bit high up, isn't it? Come on, we'd better get on with it.'

He advanced a few feet and then stared in amazement. On the floor, man-sized and dressed in chain mail and helmet, was a body. Just for a moment Tennant thought it was real and then realized by the limp manner in which it lay that it was merely a man of straw. Here was the dummy that Adam Gillow should have thrown over while the man whom it represented – himself – ducked beneath the parapet.

'How come nobody spotted this before, Potter? I mean what about the other knight – Robin Green? Surely he must have seen it still lying there before he made his exit?'

'I should imagine, sir, that the shock of falling over backwards which probably dislodged his helmet must have rendered him almost blind. And by the time he recovered himself the lights must have gone down on the scene and he had to concentrate like mad to get down the spiral in the dimness.'

'In other words, he didn't see it.'

'No, and he was on his own up here, wasn't he? Wasn't he?'

'That remains to be seen,' answered Tennant grimly.

'And did nobody else come up? Later, I mean.'

'Again. We'll have to find out.'

He walked over to it and leant over the battlements. Below him was the courtyard and the doctor just getting to her feet. He could also see two men with a body bag approaching the mortal remains of Gerry Harlington. So it ends for all of us, he thought. But hopefully not in such a violent manner.

Potter, sidling along, was searching the battlements on his hands and knees. He exclaimed, then said, 'Take a look at these, sir.'

Tennant bent to see. On the wall, beneath the parapet at knee and foot height were marks where somebody had kicked the bricks violently.

'Looks like signs of a struggle.'

'Yes, I would say so. If somebody attacked the late Mr Harlington from behind, came on him unexpectedly and pushed him hard . . .'

'He would have kicked out and fought as they tipped him towards the parapet.'

'I know the guy who was fighting him had fallen on his backside but surely he could have staggered up and intervened.'

'A very good point, Potter. I think we must go and interview him fast.'

They scoured the rest of the battlement area but found no further evidence other than a matted piece of fur that looked as if it had been torn from an ancient fur coat. It was stuck on the parapet. Tennant put it in an evidence bag, then said, 'Get the photographer and the forensic team up here, Potter. I want these marks photographed and analysed. If they were caused by scuffling feet then I think we can say that this was a murder.'

'Right you are.'

Potter made his way back down the spiral with a look of relief on his face. Tennant meanwhile walked along the battlements, taking in the full beauty of Fulke Castle. Far below him he saw Rufus Beaudegrave get into a Jaguar sports car and drive over the causeway, through the gatehouse to the open countryside beyond.

Tennant walked back slowly to the place where the straw body lay and stood there silently thinking. Then he crossed the space between the two staircases and, opening the door, went down the second one. He descended the stairs carefully, one slow step at a time, and eventually his patience was rewarded.

Lying near the bottom, half hidden by the shadow of the spiral was a rather smart fountain pen. Slipping on a protective glove Tennant picked it up and dropped it into an evidence bag. Expensive though it was, it was still run of the mill and could have belonged to anyone. With a sigh he stepped out of the darkness and into the autumn sunshine, looking for Sergeant Potter.

TWELVE

Ekaterina stared blankly at the two police officers – a man and a woman – who stood opposite her in the living room of the moated manor.

'You say Gerry is dead?' she asked them in a dazed manner.

'Yes, Mrs Harlington. I'm afraid he is,' the WPC answered her quietly. 'Why don't you sit down? Can I get you a cup of tea, perhaps?'

'No, nothing thank you. But how did this happen? Where is his body? Surely he cannot have died by his own hand.'

Her Russian accent and phraseology were becoming more pronounced in her apparent distress.

'We really don't know, Mrs Harlington,' said the man. 'Your husband was found at Fulke Castle. From what we have been told he took part in a theatrical production there and met with some kind of accident.'

Ekaterina went white as a sail. 'In that case he must have been killed,' she croaked in a voice so ghastly that it would have made an ordinary person shudder, though not so the stoical members of the police force.

'Please don't jump to conclusions, madam,' said the WPC. 'Nobody knows at the moment. We are making enquiries.'

'But I was at the castle last night,' Ekaterina stated, sitting down hard on the sofa. 'I didn't see anything happen. Gerry wasn't in it. You must be mistaken.'

'I don't think so, Mrs Harlington,' said the male police officer firmly. 'Your husband has been identified by someone who knew him. Now, have you any friends locally? Somebody who could come and stay with you perhaps?'

'I am new here. I only know my masseur and the cleaning lady. Oh, and the vicar.'

'Then perhaps we could phone one of them for you. What is the vicar's number?'

'It is on the pad by the telephone,' Ekaterina answered quietly.

She was stunned by the news but didn't truly believe it. She had known Gerry Harlington too long and too well to believe that he would actually allow himself to be murdered. In fact she expected him to walk through the front door at any minute and tell the police to get lost. Yet she had to admit that he had been strangely absent ever since the dress rehearsal and that was one thing she couldn't quite explain. Added to this had been her sudden panic this morning that had culminated in her phoning Rufus, only for her to get the answerphone. She had not left a message.

She vaguely became aware of the chime of the front door and heard the woman police officer go to answer it. A second later the man she was thinking of actually strode in.

'Oh, my dear,' he said.

And with those words she knew that everything was true.

*   *   *

Tennant and Potter were sitting in their car, parked outside a rather austere Victorian villa, situated in a side road running off Oakbridge High Street. They were waiting for the return of Robin Green who, so they had been informed by his next-door neighbour, had gone off early with the Wayfarers Wanderlust Association.

'He's generally home by six 'cos he likes to watch the news. I can hear it through my wall.'

Tennant had raised a saddened eyebrow. 'Why, oh why, my dear Potter, do we always have to wait for those we most need to speak to?'

'Sod's law, sir.'

'A truer word was never spoken.'

They sat in silence, Potter chewing on a Double Whopper burger, Tennant wishing he hadn't given up smoking and biting furiously on a Polo mint. It grew dark and the inspector was just glancing at his watch when they heard the sound of sensible footsteps and the figure of a man in brown shorts worn over skinny legs, together with an enormous pair of walking boots and grey knee socks, appeared through the gloom. Tennant was out of the car in a flash leaving Potter to swallow the remainder of his Double Whopper in an indigestible lump.

'Mr Robin Green?'

'Yes,' said the figure, peering suspiciously.

'Inspector Dominic Tennant, Sussex Police. We'd like to ask you a few questions please.' Tennant flashed his badge.

'Oh dear, yes. Is it about the dustbins?'

Tennant smiled. 'May we come in for a second? It's getting rather cold out here.'

They made their way into a truly boring living room furnished in shades of Elephant's Breath grey. Robin pulled the dusty curtains and, turning a switch, a nasty and unappetizing electric fire came on with imitation coals giving off a feeble flicker.

'Take a seat please. Can I get you anything?'

They both refused though Tennant was sorely tempted to say 'A large vodka please.'

'Now, gentlemen, what can I do for you?'

Is it possible, the inspector thought, that he doesn't know? He asked a question of his own.

'What time did you leave this morning?'

'About seven. We ramblers set off earlier in the summer but these autumn mornings can be a bit sharp.'

'Then you probably haven't heard the news.'

'What news?' Robin looked nervous, like a startled rat.

'I'm afraid Gerry Harlington is dead. He fell over the parapet during the very scene in which you were involved, Mr Green. Because you were not fighting Adam Gillow but Harlington. I am referring of course to the duel on the battlements which took place last night in the Son et Lumière at Fulke Castle.'

'The one in which you unfortunately fell down,' put in Potter acerbically.

Robin had gone a horrible shade of yellow, which was not pleasant to look at.

'You remember the fight, no doubt.'

'I'll say I do. That fall was no accident I can tell you. Somebody reached out of the door behind me and poked me in the legs with a stick. It threw me off balance and I fell over.'

Tennant felt his heartbeat quicken and beside him he was aware of Potter leaning forward.

'Who was it? Did you see them?'

'I couldn't see anything. The fall disengaged my helmet and I was plunged into darkness. By the time I pulled it back straight the dummy had gone over and I had to make my way out in the pitch black.'

'Tell me what you heard.'

'Well, not much. I thought a door opened . . .'

'Which one? Behind you or in front?'

'I can't be sure. I was very confused but I thought it was the one in front. Somebody poking me with a stick had quite upset me.'

'We're relying on you to help us. Please, Mr Green,' said Potter.

'I repeat, I think it was the door in front of me. After that I thought I heard a bit of a scuffle but the tape was playing loudly at that moment, my helmet had fallen over my eyes and I was generally concentrating on other things. And that is all I have to say.'

'Did you hear a scream?'

'There was a scream loud enough to waken the dead on the tape. But now you come to mention it I thought I heard a shout nearer at hand.'

Tennant looked at Potter.

'You do realize, Mr Green, that we will have to ask you to come to Lewes and make a statement to this effect.'

'Yes, I do. And I have something to say to you. No doubt you will have heard that I jumped on Gerry Harlington at the dress rehearsal after he had done that obscene dance during the Elizabethan Fair scene. But I can assure you, Inspector, that I had no hand in his death. I disliked the man intensely, believed he was a beastly braggart . . .'

How quaint, thought Tennant, concealing a small smile.

'. . . but for all my feelings I could not murder anybody. To take a life is quite beyond me.'

'But you attacked the man two nights ago.'

'That was different,' answered Robin. 'He was trying to ruin what I considered to be a work of art.'

'Be that as it may you still had no time for him.'

'But last night I thought I was fighting Adam,' said Robin, a note of hysteria entering his tone. 'I couldn't see his face and I believed it was him. Oh my God, you must realize that.'

Tennant rose to his feet. 'Right. You can put all this in a statement. We'll see you at Lewes at ten o'clock tomorrow morning. Don't be late, Mr Green.'

Once outside Tennant turned to Potter, smiling a little wryly.

'Well, we've got a murder on our hands if old shorty pants is to be believed.'

'*Do* you believe him, sir?'

'It's all feasible, of course. But the question remains how could somebody come through the door behind him, knock his legs with a stick, run down the spiral stairs, mount the other staircase, come through the other door and heave Harlington over the parapet?'

'You mean there were two of them?'

'It looks like it.'

'Or he's telling a pack of lies and did it himself.'

'Which is far more probable.' Tennant looked at his watch. 'Is it too late to call on the vicar of Lakehurst?'

'And perhaps drop in at The Great House?' answered Potter with a smile.

'Pity you're driving,' answered the inspector as the car started up.

It seemed to Nick Lawrence that he had been on the phone all morning, either ringing out or receiving calls. Paul Silas had been the second to phone at approximately ten o'clock. Before that there had been a call from a policewoman asking if it would it be possible for him to visit Mrs Harlington who was in a state of shock.

'Why?' Nick had asked.

'Oh, I'm sorry, Vicar. The fact is Mr Harlington died last night.'

'Good God. How did it happen? Was he involved in an accident?'

'In a manner of speaking, yes, sir. Will you be able to visit?'

'Yes, of course. Tell her I'll be there at about eleven o'clock.'

Half an hour later Paul had come through.

'Hello, Reverend Nick. How are you?'

'I'm very well thank you. What's all this I hear about Gerry Harlington?'

'My dear chap there's a fine how-do-you-do. The castle has been closed off as a scene of crime and has policemen standing guard and apparently some high falutin' police inspector from Lewes is taking charge.'

'So what has happened exactly?'

'It seems that he – Gerry that is – was up on the battlements last night fighting Robin Green and pitched over the balustrade and plunged to his death.'

'Did he fall or was he pushed?' said Nick, quoting an ancient saying.

'That's the burning question. Nobody seems to know as yet.'

'You don't think Robin . . .?'

'No, I don't actually. Because he really was under the impression it was Adam Gillow up there. I mean, you can't recognize anyone behind those damn helmets.'

'So . . .?'

'So, my dear friend, the show is pulled, cancelled. I rang

the chief constable – we're both members of the same Masonic lodge you know – and he told me that it was utterly impossible to proceed at least for the next few days. I'm sorry but there 'tis.'

The next call had been from Jonquil Charmwood.

'Help, Nick. What on earth's going on?'

'Jonquil, I didn't see you in the pub last night. Nor, funnily enough, in the last scene. Did you have to leave early?'

'Er, no. I mean yes. But what's all this I hear about the show being pulled?'

'Well it seems that Gerry Harlington met with an accident.'

'Gerry? What was he doing there? I thought he had walked out of the whole thing.'

'Apparently not. It was him fighting up on the battlements with Robin Green. I don't know how but it appears he fell off and was killed.'

Nick heard Jonquil draw breath and then there was a long silence.

'But surely the show must go on.'

'The police are treating the death as suspicious. They have marked the castle as a crime scene and there is no chance in the world of any of us getting near it.'

There was another long pause and then Jonquil said breathlessly, 'Nick, are you free to come and have supper with me one evening?'

'Why, yes. Thank you very much. When would be convenient?'

'Any night this week, though we had better make it earlier rather than later just in case the show goes on again.'

Small hope of that, thought Nick.

To Jonquil he said, 'Well, how about Wednesday?'

'That would be fine.'

'What time shall I come?'

'About seven thirty. You have my address, don't you.'

Nick put the phone down and looked at his watch. It was getting on for eleven and he had arranged to call on Ekaterina. Hurriedly he put on his dog collar and dark shirt and made his way outside to the car.

*   *   *

By the time the evening came the vicar was well and truly ready for a pint. He had found Ekaterina pale but not weeping, being comforted by Sir Rufus Beaudegrave. Nick had been somewhat surprised by this, not realizing that the couple even knew one another. But he had taken it in his stride and had accepted Ekaterina's offer of some coffee.

They had carried it outside, for though chilly the sun was warming the courtyard and it was good to leave the house in which the essence of Gerry Harlington seemed omnipresent.

'Why don't you get away for a few days, Mrs Harlington? It would do you good,' Nick had observed, gazing out at the moat and the countryside beyond and thinking how heavenly the whole setting was.

'I've invited Ekaterina to come and stay whenever she feels like it,' Rufus had answered.

In a flash of inspiration Nick had realized that the man had already fallen hopelessly in love with Gerry's widow and had felt tremendously pleased for them. Then he had reproved himself, thinking of the horror of the Wasp Man's painful and terrible death.

'Have the police been to see you yet?' he had asked.

Ekaterina had turned her beautiful face to him. 'Not to interview me, no. I had a phone call from one of them. He was an inspector. He had a nice voice and was well spoken. He is coming to see me tomorrow.'

Nick had suddenly looked up. 'His name wasn't Tennant by any chance?'

She had stared at him. 'Yes, it was. Do you know him?'

'Indeed I do. He's a very good man.'

Sir Rufus had spoken. 'Then I hope he solves the case quickly and finds out that it was all a tragic accident.'

'Yes,' Nick had replied thoughtfully.

Rufus had picked up on it. 'You don't think it was?'

'To be perfectly honest with you I don't know.'

'Well I can give Ekaterina an alibi, should anyone ask. We were together watching the show from the Tudor banqueting hall the entire evening. Plus my four daughters. We had a very cosy time.'

Ekaterina sighed. 'It was a pity that such beauty could mask such tragedy.'

THIRTEEN

The Great House was heaving with people all talking loudly; the jungle drums had definitely been beating regarding the strange events at Fulke Castle and for a minute the inspector wondered how. Then he thought that this was a true example of village life and simply accepted it.

Jack Boggis was sitting in his usual seat, his newspaper lying before him on the table, listening for once to old Alfred who was holding forth with animation about the show he had seen at the castle and the tragic events that had followed it. Boggis looked up as Tennant and Potter came in and flashed his set of mighty false teeth in what was supposed to be a welcoming smile.

'Hello, Inspector, I expect you're here on business.'

'Good evening, Mr Boggis. Yes, you could say that. Were you in the audience the other night? I'm talking about the Son et Lumière at Fulke Castle.'

'Me? No fear. You wouldn't catch me going to one of those damned amateur shows. I'd rather sit at home with the telly. Personally I'm a great admirer of Sally Grey, pretty little thing. And I like Robert Newton as well. They're more my cup of tea.'

Tennant exchanged a look with his sergeant and murmured, 'Talk about revealing your age.'

'Yes, indeed, sir.'

Alfred was piping up. 'I was there, Inspector. I enjoyed it very much indeed.' This with a self-satisfied glance at Jack. 'It was extremely colourful and well done. But I never noticed anything was wrong. The dummy that turned out to be Mr Harlington went over ever so convincingly.'

'Was there anything peculiar about the fall? A scream for instance?'

Potter couldn't help but notice that Boggis was adopting an amused grin, the way that people do when listening to a garrulous child.

'No, not really. It was very loud but that was all on the tape, of course. But now I can't help wondering if the sound wasn't boosted by a real cry of terror.'

'Thank you Mr . . .?'

'Alfred Munn, sir. And I live at Parsley Cottage, West Street, Lakehurst.'

'Thank you so much. Have you got all that Potter? We'll be in touch again should we need anything further. Now, where's the vicar?'

'He's over there talking to that wop.' Boggis had got his chance and was speaking up extremely loudly.

'I beg your pardon?'

'He's talking to that wop – that Italian. Now he's the man you should be looking out for, Inspector. Comes over here, a real Johnny-come-lately, stays at the pub without telling anyone his business. Then before you can say Jack Robinson he's in that bloody Son et Lumière just as if he owns the bloody place. Damned Eyeties. I haven't trusted 'em since the war.'

'Fortunately for the United Nations not many people share your view these days,' remarked Potter.

They made their way to the centre of the bar where a hub of people had formed round the vicar and Ricardo, who were the very pinnacle of attention.

The masseur, aware of his good figure and sleek, dark looks was describing the scene at the Son et Lumière to those who hadn't already been there. He rolled his gorgeous eyes and gesticulated and his resonant voice carried with the words 'But, my friends, I can assure you that we in the show knew nothing. Nothing at all. Not till this morning did I receive a call from Ekaterina telling me not to come. That there had been a terrible accident.'

'What exactly do you do for Mrs Harlington?' asked Giles Fielding, a Sussex sheep farmer, who was sitting on a bar stool taking it all in.

'I was her masseur,' Ricardo answered with pride.

'Aye aye,' said another voice meaningfully.

'Which parts of her did you massage?' said somebody else.

'Sir, that is a slight on my profession.'

'Now calm down boys,' put in Nick. 'There's no need to be vulgar. We've told you as much as we know about what happened. Gerry Harlington went hurtling over the battlements, pushed by some unseen hand. But whose hand it was is yet to be discovered.'

Behind him he felt a stirring and the next second he turned round and looked straight into the face of his old friend, Dominic Tennant, accompanied by that most respectable young man, Mark Potter.

Nick held out his hand.

'My dear Inspector, how marvellous to see you. I presume you're here about what took place the other night?'

Tennant nodded. 'I am indeed. Now how many present were members of the Son et Lumière cast?' he asked.

The vicar and Ricardo put their hands up, as did a couple of other people, a wispy man and a hatchet-faced woman who looked as if they would enjoy folkish activities.

'Shall we find a seat in a quiet corner – that is if there is such a thing in this place,' suggested Tennant.

'There's a table over there,' said Potter. 'A party is just leaving.' And he shot off and grabbed it before anyone could argue.

They all sat round and the two Lakehurst people introduced themselves as Joyce and Lewis Partridge.

'And what were your roles in the show?' Tennant asked while Potter silently removed his notebook.

'I played Piers Gaveston,' said Lewis with a certain pride.

'Wasn't he gay?' asked Potter.

'Well, he was bisexual, certainly.'

'To say nothing of Hugh Despenser,' Potter answered surprisingly.

'I too am sometimes of the gay persuasion,' said Lewis. 'And my wife does not object, do you dear.'

'I think people's sexuality is entirely up to the individual,' Joyce replied in irritating nasal tones that went through Tennant like a knife. He could imagine her scrubbing out their clothes by hand and then pegging them on an old rope line, all this whilst playing an accordion.

No wonder, he thought, that her husband has other interests.

'Tell me, if you will, whether either of you noticed anything unusual about the performance of the Son et Lumière.'

'Yes, I did,' answered Joyce, 'several things.'

'Such as?'

She leant forward in a confidential manner and the inspector noticed for the first time that she had two long plaits which hung down to her waist, one of which swung to the side as she began to talk earnestly.

'Well, other than for the fact that Adam Gillow was missing – though I didn't notice that at the time – it was the behaviour of the bear that I thought odd.'

'The bear?' exclaimed Potter, lowering his notebook.

'Yes. It arrived really early, before any of the rest of us got there, and was in full costume – head and all – wandering about for ages.'

'I see. But what was so unusual about that?'

'The part was played by Jonquil Charmwood. She's a modern-day equivalent of a bright young thing. She always rushes in at the last minute and dives into her costume, puts the head in place just before she is due on then hurries up to the bear tamer and away she goes. But this night she just behaved differently.'

'I see,' Tennant said. 'But surely she was on stage before the Elizabethan Fair?'

'No, that's just the point – she wasn't. It's because her costume was so complicated that the director – and I speak of Bob Merryfield not that small-time actor – let her off. The Fair was her first appearance.'

'I take it you didn't like Gerry Harlington,' remarked Potter.

Lewis spoke up. 'It is not that we have anything against anyone of whatever race, creed, colour or sexual inclination.'

Pompous little ass, thought Tennant.

'Quite so,' he said aloud, and caught the vicar's eye, which was twinkling.

'But Gerry Harlington was more than one could stomach. So pretentious. And on what basis?'

'I thought he was jolly good as the Wasp Man – at least my nephews did,' put in Potter.

Lewis looked down his long aquiline nose. 'Precisely.'

The vicar interrupted. 'He had talent. One can't take that away from him. That hip-hop dance he did at the dress rehearsal was really excellent. It was just totally out of place. I don't think he had much idea of English history.'

'You can say that again, Reverend,' said Joyce. 'He was a total ignoramus.'

'Can we get back to the subject of the bear, please. What happened after she finished her scene?'

'Well, that's just the point. Nobody saw her go. And she didn't appear in any of the last acts. She was meant to be in the big Charleston number but she never showed up. It was too bad.'

'And what happened to her costume?'

'It was found, neat as you please, hanging up on a hanger on Sir Rufus's estate car.'

'Really? He never mentioned that.'

'He didn't see it. It was removed by one of the stagehands and put back in our changing tent.'

'And how do you know all this?'

''Cos I saw him put it back and asked him where he found it,' Joyce answered triumphantly, and glugged down her Gold Label with a knowing air.

'Well, thank you very much for the information. Potter, make a note that I will be interviewing Miss Charmwood myself.'

The vicar said a little uncomfortably, 'I'm going to have dinner with her tomorrow night. I can ask her about it if you like.'

Tennant's eyebrow rose and he looked pixieish. 'How very kind of you. But I shall be seeing her nonetheless.'

'Yes,' said Nick, a trifle sheepishly, 'I thought you would.'

Afterwards in the comforting walls of the vicarage, Nick sat down to watch the ten o'clock news. There was a piece on national television about the strange death at Fulke Castle and how the police were investigating. There was also a short inclusion on Gerry's widow, Ekaterina, saying she had been born in Russia, followed by a brief bit of footage of herself and Gerry going to a Hollywood premiere.

Nick thought about tomorrow night and the fact that Jonquil had issued the invitation rather than him asking her. Then Olivia came into his head and he was glad that she was missing the drama of this particular investigation. He yawned and stood up. Above his head, William walked across the landing and Radetsky simultaneously came through the cat flap. The vicar smiled. All was well. He could go to bed.

*   *   *

But there was to be no early night for Dominic Tennant. Before he had parted company with Joyce and Lewis he had obtained a full list of everyone involved in the first-night performance both on and backstage. Sir Rufus had already given him a programme but this was nothing like as comprehensive as the slightly malicious gossip emanating from the folksy pair.

'Of course, it's poor Oswald I feel sorry for. He took the post hoping he would learn more about directing,' Joyce had said spitefully. 'But he was treated like dirt – that is by Mr Harlington. He was nothing more than a gofer.'

'How old was he?' Tennant had asked.

'Nineteen. But very introspective. Wouldn't speak up for himself except in monosyllables. You know the type.'

Unfortunately the inspector did and made another mental note to interview him personally and to be firm with the youth.

Tennant, at last home in his lovely flat, finished his lists and turned to his own mail which lay in an untouched heap on his desk. There was a postcard with a Chinese stamp and he wondered momentarily who could have sent it. Then he remembered that Olivia was on a world tour. He opened it and skimmed through the lines. Then re-read it slowly. The last bit amused and pleased him.

Hope there are no more grisly happenings in downtown Lakehurst! Give my love to all and sundry but save a little for yourself, Olivia.

The inspector went to bed that night with a smile on his face.

FOURTEEN

The smile was wiped off Tennant's face when the alarm clock rang at six. By seven he was suited and booted and had made his way into police headquarters where he sat at his desk and waited for his team to arrive for a briefing at eight o'clock. Lately he had been cultivating something of an image for himself as he was frequently approached to appear on television. He had let his dark hair grow slightly and had enhanced his natural curls by the clever use of gel. His suits – made by a tailor in Brighton who charged reasonable prices – were often in lighter shades, contrasting well with his flowing overcoat; he had worn the same one for the last two years and was quite famous for it. He chose colourful ties, often with a vivid pattern of flowers. Gone was the plodding policeman of yesteryear. Tennant spoke well, was articulate, friendly, and capable of flashing the odd attractive grin. He was extremely popular with both BBC and Meridian interviewers.

Reliable Potter turned up at ten to eight and was followed by a dozen or so members of Tennant's team, all looking ready to go. These included a female detective with thick dark lashes and wood-violet eyes and a fiancé, much to the chagrin of the younger males. Her name was Morgana Driscoll and her partner was a police constable on the beat, which secretly amused some of the more senior people, though not Tennant who inclined to the theory that they were all members of the same service regardless of their rank.

He outlined a detailed account of what had taken place at Fulke Castle, handed out lists of people to be interviewed and told them to get on with it. He would see them again tomorrow morning, same time and the best of luck. Then he and Potter went downstairs to the car and headed for the mortuary in which lay the last mortal remains of Gerry Harlington.

'I asked a Home Office pathologist to do this one, Potter.'

'Very wise, sir.'

The body was lying on a metal table covered with a white cloth and the pathologist, Dr Bernard Lance, was at the sink washing his hands. In death what was left of Gerry's face seemed as if it were frozen in ice, as if a mask had descended over his features, draining them of all reality. Tennant felt that they were looking at a black doll, a dark representation of someone who had once lived and breathed and been a film star. Just for a second he felt tremendously sorry for the man and then his profession-alism took over and he turned to the pathologist.

'Well, Dr Lance. How are you today?'

'Very fit, dear boy. So we have the Wasp Man, eh?'

'Yes. Did you ever see any of his films?'

'Saw them all. My daughter was an avid fan and d'you know

I got to quite like the feller. He was very athletic, I'll say that for him. Leaping about, swinging on ropes, sword fighting. The lot.'

Potter who was just putting on his protective gown said, 'I'd agree with that, sir. I was quite taken with him myself.'

'Pity he had to end like this.'

Tennant asked, 'Just exactly how did he die?'

'Massive injuries to the cranium, of course, brought about by his fall. But have a look at this. Should be of interest.'

Dr Lance called for two assistants who proceeded to turn the body over. Tennant was horribly aware of the movement of a hip-hop dancer, turning on one arm, looking up at the crowd, broad grin on face. He gave the smallest shudder and momentarily wondered if he was too imaginative for the job. Meanwhile Dr Lance was pointing to bruises, no bigger than a hand-span, on the dead man's waist.

'What do you make of those?' asked the pathologist as if he were questioning a group of students.

Tennant and Potter leaned in closely and had a look.

'Push marks?' the sergeant asked.

'I would say so,' answered his boss. They both turned to the pathologist.

'No doubt about it in my mind. It seems to me that someone came up behind the unfortunate Wasp Man and gave him a hard push which sent him stumbling to his death.'

'There was some sort of scuffle following the fight up on the battlements but unfortunately the other person involved had fallen down and jammed his helmet on his head so he couldn't see a damn thing. That is if he's telling the truth.'

'Looks as if he is, sir. I don't see how he could have whipped round behind the victim and given him a hearty shove and then got back into his place again. Not considering the time factor.'

'You're right of course. So –' Tennant straightened up – 'we must go hunting. And if we work on the theory of who stood to gain then there is only one obvious person.'

'The wife,' said Potter.

And Tennant nodded his head.

*   *   *

Before they drove back to Lakehurst the inspector had one call to make. For there was an important person connected with the Oakhurst Dramatists and Dramatic Society who was at present studying at the South Downs College of Further Education in Lewes. Young Oswald Souter was there doing a drama course. At approximately eleven o'clock the two policemen drove up outside the place and actually managed to find a parking space, then went straight to the principal's office.

It was discovered that Oswald was presently on a short break in the canteen from which he was duly fetched out. He arrived in the small office that had been found for Tennant, appearing pale and puzzled. The inspector immediately felt sorry for him.

Oswald was an ordinary-looking boy, medium height, medium build and inclined to acne. Tennant, who in the past had had longings to go on the stage, could only see him playing character roles in the years that lay ahead. The poor youth was also painfully thin and had several zits on his face at which he had clearly picked. He was clutching a packet of half-eaten sandwiches in his hand and the inspector felt like telling him to finish them off and build himself up a bit.

'Come in, Oswald, and take a seat. Now this is really nothing to worry about. I just want to talk about the performance of Son et Lumière the other night if that's all right with you.'

Potter flicked open his notebook.

'What do you want to know about it?' asked the lad, his Adam's apple bobbing ferociously.

'I understand you were assistant director.'

'Yes, that's right.'

God, he's going to be one of those, thought Tennant. I'm going to have to drag the facts out of the little pest.

'And how did you get on with that?'

'Very well under Mr Merryfield.'

'Go on.'

'But he died unexpectedly and Gerry Harlington took over.'

'Yes, I know. So how did you get on with him?'

Oswald blushed slowly, starting with his neck then the colour working its way up to his sparrow-coloured hair.

'Not so well.'

'It has been said to me that he treated you as a gofer. Would that be correct?'

'Yes.'

Potter interrupted. 'Look, Oswald, why don't you tell the inspector the whole story. You're going to be here all day if you go on as slowly as this.'

Oswald gulped and his Adam's apple did a nosedive.

'Well, what do you want to know?'

'Tell me about the performance of Son et Lumière. It was your role to take the dummy up to the battlements, wasn't it? Now can you describe the details of what happened that night. Recount to me exactly what took place.'

'All right. I got there early because that was what I was supposed to do. There was nobody around except for the bear. I waved at her – it was Jonquil, you see – and she waved a paw back. I went to collect the dummy from where it was lying under the arches . . .'

'How did you know it would be thrown there?'

'Because that was what Adam Gillow always did. He ducked down and simultaneously threw the dummy over the parapet. It landed in roughly the same place every rehearsal. Besides, it was up to Charlie Higgs to move it under the arches.'

'Go on.'

'Well, it was there all right. So I picked it up and took it up the spiral staircase and placed it just under the parapet out of sight. Then I went back down and that is all I can tell you.'

'And you did not go near the battlements again that night?'

'No.'

'Did anybody else?'

'No.'

'What did you wear during the performance?'

'Black. I had some black jeans belonging to my father, a black T-shirt and some trainers that I'd put boot polish on. Why?'

It was the first question that Oswald had asked and it rather startled Tennant.

'I just wondered what the backstage crew wore. Whether you had cloaks or anything to blend with the actors.'

'I think there were one or two cloaks lying about. I never wore one if that's what you're asking.'

Tennant shook his head. 'Well, thank you, Mr Souter. You've been very helpful. There's just one other thing.'

'What's that?'

'Did you see anybody go near the battlements or up one of the spiral staircases on the night that Gerry Harlington was murdered? In short, did you see anything out of place happen at all?'

'I didn't see anything. I just got on with my job.'

'Well, thank you again. Sorry to have interrupted you at college but we were saving petrol.'

Potter grinned but Oswald's face remained impassive.

'Can I go?'

'Certainly. We have your home address. We'll be in touch if we need anything further.'

He held the door open and Oswald marched through, sandwich box still clutched in hand.

'Uncommunicative little bugger,' Tennant said, looking at the young man's retreating form.

'I can't imagine him and the Wasp Man hitting it off. Not the type at all.'

'Oh well, it takes all sorts. Come on, Potter. We've a mountain to get through today.'

They drove on to Speckled Wood and Tennant asked Potter to stop the car so that they might look at the view. It was quite indescribable with the autumn colours beginning to gleam in the foliage. To their right lay the livery stables that had once been the scene of such sadness but which now had a bright and bustling air about them. Above them lay the ancient farmhouse and the land owned by Giles Fielding on which grazed mild-mannered sheep, moving slowly over the fields as they cropped the grass. Tennant had briefly lived opposite a sheep field and had forever been nipping over the stile and pulling them out when they got their heads stuck in the hedge. When he thought about it now it seemed as if it had been in another life. He had been married, had been briefly happy before his wife had run off with her actor lover – amateur of course. He had been a different person.

Tennant turned his eyes to the distant view. There glittered that tantalizing cobalt glimpse of the sea, the woods and pastures sweeping down to it, the land the colour of sage and parsley. At this time of day, with the autumn sun low in the sky, the water in the moat of the house which Tennant had always longed to have glinted dazzlingly so that one had to shade one's eyes in order to look at it.

'There's the house I've always fancied living in, Potter.'

'Well you'll have to chat up the Wasp Man's missus then.'

They drove down a narrow lane, plunging into the verdant countryside, at one point the trees leaning over and forming an arch above their heads. The leaves were just beginning to turn colour so that a ripple of red and gold was visible here and there. Tennant could not help but think that autumn was one of the loveliest times of the year, a time when people settled down and took stock of their lives. He thought of Olivia's postcard and decided that as soon as she returned to England he would phone and invite her out to dinner.

The door was opened by Ekaterina Harlington looking pale but exquisite in Versace. Tennant introduced himself and Potter did likewise, following her into the glorious room that led off the hallway, the inspector looking admiringly round him. His sergeant, on the other hand, could not take his eyes off the woman they had come to interview and hardly noticed his surroundings.

'Please sit down,' she said. 'Would you like something to drink? I have coffee, tea, or something stronger. Which would you prefer?'

'Coffee for me, please,' Tennant answered, while Potter – who could not take the expression of total admiration from his face – asked for tea.

'A minute,' said Ekaterina, who rose and disappeared for a second or two.

'Potter,' Tennant whispered, 'remove that look for pity's sake. You're like a schoolboy watching an X film.'

'I feel like one. What a woman!'

'No doubt. But remember we are here on official business.'

Ekaterina returned followed by a bustling cleaning lady carrying a tray of cups and plates, followed a second or two later by a small boy bearing a teapot and a cafetière.

'He is her son,' said Ekaterina in an undertone. Then, loudly,

'Thank you, Callum,' when he returned bearing cakes. She turned to the inspector. 'You have come, no doubt, about the death of my husband.'

'Yes, madam. I don't know how to put this any other way but the fact is that Mr Harlington was deliberately pushed over the parapet. In other words, his death was not accidental.'

'I see. Well, I am not altogether surprised.'

Potter flipped open his notebook.

'You see, Gerry was one of those people who made enemies wherever he went. The trouble was that he suffered with an overpowering ego. He always thought that he knew best and could do things better than anyone else. The fact that one day he would be murdered was almost a foregone conclusion.'

'You speak of it very matter-of-factly, if you don't mind my saying so.'

Ekaterina raised an exquisite shoulder. 'How do you want me to say it? I will be honest with you. I fell out of love with him years ago and only the other day I decided on a divorce. Does that make me a suspect? I suppose it does. Do have a cake please. Mrs Wills has baked them freshly.'

Tennant smiled to himself. Working on the old who-stood-to-gain-most method Mrs Harlington had to be suspect number one. But he believed she had an alibi for that night given by Rufus Beaudegrave himself. Nevertheless, it was his duty to probe.

'Well, Mrs Harlington, in order to eliminate you from our enquiries I am obliged to ask you a few questions.'

'Ask away.' She sipped green tea from an expensive-looking cup.

'Are you the dead man's only relative? Has he had any children by this or any other marriage?'

She smiled at him kindly. 'You are trying to find out if I am going to inherit Gerry's vast fortune, I suppose. The truth is, Inspector Tennant, that he did not have one. He had blown all the money he ever earned on failed and dismal projects in the theatre. For example, his soap opera. It was completely and utterly useless. They showed it at midnight in the US. In Britain it wasn't shown at all. Then he tried an 'I Will Make You a Star' venture which was aired on the Internet. A few pathetic black girls took their bras off and waved their goods in the faces of the cameras.

He lost thousands on that project. Other than for the Wasp Man movies, Gerry was a walking disaster.'

Tennant put his cup down and stretched out his arms. 'But this house, the cars I saw parked outside . . . they must have cost a fortune.'

Ekaterina shrugged. 'But I bought them all.'

'You?'

'Yes, you see I was the late Grigori Makarichoff's only child.'

Potter spluttered into his tea cup and Tennant grew very still.

'You mean that you were – are – the billionaire oligarch's daughter?'

'Yes,' said Ekaterina, 'I am. So you see I hold the purse strings.'

'I'll say you do, by God,' answered Tennant forcefully.

FIFTEEN

I t was evening and Nick Lawrence, attired in casual clothes he had bought off the peg whilst on holiday in Italy – hoping that they made him look debonair and sophisticated – got into his car, which he kept parked permanently in West Street as the vicarage did not run to a garage. He had bought an attractive bunch of flowers and had also carefully selected a bottle of wine, and armed with these was making his way to Oakbridge and his dinner date with Jonquil Charmwood.

He had to confess it, he found the young woman extremely attractive in an offhand sort of way. She had all the attributes that he liked: nice hair, large expressive eyes, a kindly mouth, but she was terribly brittle in the modern style of her sex. She was one of those girls who seemed to be constantly in a hurry, dashing from one thing to the next. Frankly, Nick had been terribly surprised to be invited to dinner and wondered whether he was merely making weight, had been called upon because he was that much sought-after thing – an extra male.

So he was astonished when arriving at her maisonette in a thirties house situated in a side street behind The George and Dragon, to discover that he was the only guest. His heart sank a little as he realized that the entire burden of conversation would fall on him. Then he remembered that at university he had been hailed as a wit and raconteur and gathered himself together.

He imagined that Jonquil would be upstairs putting the finishing touches to her make-up and that he would hear her light quick step come running down the staircase and the door would be opened with a flourish. But instead he could have sworn that she was hovering in the hall and had opened the door while he was still straightening his Armani jacket.

'Oh, hello, Vicar. Do come in.'

'Thanks, Jonquil. By the way, you must call me Nick. All my friends do.'

He produced the bouquet of flowers and gave it to her with one of his odd little bows. She smiled but he couldn't help but notice that some of her customary zest was missing.

'Why thank you. You really shouldn't have.'

'My pleasure. It was kind of you to ask me. I've brought some wine as well.'

'Goodness. You are spoiling me. Come into the living room and sit down. I've got some wine cooling in there.'

The room was small and reminded Nick of many he had seen like it, a typical thirties layout, modernized by Jonquil's feminine touches. The old gas fire had been removed and in its place was an electric fire that represented blazing coals. Nick, addicted as he was to open blazes, thought that this was the next best thing.

Jonquil came into the room bearing a tray of snacks, which she began to place in various vantage points.

'These are to keep you going until we eat,' she said cheerfully, but underneath her bonhomie Nick could have sworn that he could sense nervousness.

Jonquil took a bottle of champagne from an ice bucket and set about wrestling with the cork.

Nick got to his feet. 'Here, allow me. I was known as Champagne Charlie at university.'

'Were you really? I've never thought of you at uni somehow.'

Nick poured two glasses. 'Well, I was. I read Medieval History. It was after I graduated that I went to study for the priesthood.'

'I don't believe in God,' said Jonquil tactlessly.

'A lot of people don't,' Nick answered sadly.

There was a slightly awkward silence broken by Jonquil suddenly getting to her feet and saying, 'Excuse me, I think I can smell something burning.'

Nick stared into the phoney coals, feeling rather depressed. He had long ago given up the idea of trying to convert someone to his way of thinking. He just knew that he had not been called to take up the priesthood but rather nudged – several times – so in the end he had had no option but to apply to an ecclesiastical college. And though he often found some of the tasks he had to perform deeply distressing – sitting with the dying, comforting the bereaved – he was more than aware that the spiritual rewards were great and he enjoyed having God as his employer, he honestly did. As for the parish of Lakehurst, he felt he was one of the luckiest souls alive to dwell in such a beautiful place and to have so charming and welcoming a vicarage.

Jonquil reappeared. 'All's well,' she said. 'Come on, Nick, pour the champagne.'

She sat down opposite him and took the glass. He noticed that her hand was shaking and that she drained its contents as quickly as possible. Neither would she look at him, but stared at the rug as if it were an old friend.

'What's the matter?' he asked eventually. 'Come on. You can tell me.'

Startlingly, she went down on her knees in front of him and threw herself into his arms. Through her convulsive tears she sobbed, 'Oh Nick, Nick, something so terrible has happened.'

'Shush, now, there there,' he said, just as if she were a weeping child. 'Just tell me all about it and we will try to sort it out.'

'But Emma's vanished,' she said, leaning back and looking at him through brooks of tears. 'She's gone – and I don't know where.'

'Emma who?' Nick asked patiently. 'Look, Jonquil, I think you had better tell me the story from the beginning.'

He helped her back into her chair, lent her a sensible hand-kerchief with the initial N in the corner – given to him by his father's girlfriend at Christmas – made shushing noises until she calmed down a little.

'It all began at that silly Son et Lumière,' Jonquil said

between sobs. 'I was suddenly presented with tickets for *Les Miserables* on the beastly thing's first night. I'd been waiting for them for ages and lo and behold they had to come on that night of all nights. Anyway, I asked a friend of mine, Emma Simms, if she'd take the part of the bear for me. In secret, of course. You see, I wanted to see *Les Mis* so badly. I know it was wrong of me but I had been waiting for months and months to get in. Then a friend of mine – who was in it by the way – got me these couple of seats and I just couldn't resist. And now Emma's gone.'

Nick stared at her in silence, his brain beginning to race.

'So what happened?' he asked.

'I don't know,' she wailed. 'Paul Silas rang me to tell me all about the murder of Gerry Harlington and then asked why I left early on the first night. I muttered something about having a headache and he said that was very unprofessional. But then I turned on the BBC news and there were pictures of Fulke Castle and a short interview with Sir Rufus, who was pleasant but obviously put out. Then there was a resumé of Gerry's career.' A small smile briefly appeared. 'Gerry was a terrible actor, wasn't he? He could dance quite well but, boy oh boy, he deserved a Smellie for the worst performances ever given.'

'But tell me about Emma. What happened to her?'

'That's just what I don't know,' Jonquil said, sniffing. 'I rang her early the next morning – that was the morning after the first night, before we knew anything bad had happened – it was at about seven thirty because she always left for work at twenty to eight – and I got her answerphone. I left a message thanking her and asking if it all went well. To cut to the chase I never got a reply. Eventually, after six or seven calls I went round there and the girl she shared the flat with told me that she hadn't clapped eyes on her since that night. She thought she'd probably gone to visit her mother unexpectedly.'

'Has this matter been reported to the police?'

'I don't honestly know. Perhaps Emma's flat mate did so.'

Nick took a swig of champagne and said, 'I think it is essential that you tell Inspector Tennant all of this tonight. I'm sure what happened to the girl is of vital importance.'

'But suppose she is with her mother? Suppose she had a call

on her mobile that her mother was ill and she must go to see her at once?'

'If that is so the police will be able to sort it out very quickly. Would you like me to ring them?'

'Oh yes. Yes please. Would you?'

Nick sighed silently, wondering why he always got the nasty jobs to do. But looking at Jonquil Charmwood, moist eyed and pleading, how could he refuse? Taking his mobile from the pocket of his Armani jacket, he dialled the number of the headquarters in Lewes.

They telephoned Tennant in his car, heading back home, thinking that a good day's work had been done. Consequently he was not pleased with the interruption and when the voice came over the loudspeaker he listened with a certain amount of irritation.

'But why wasn't the girl reported missing earlier?' he asked.

'Don't know, sir. It's all a convoluted tale. Apparently the girl genuinely playing the bear didn't want to own up at first that she went to the theatre in London.'

'Silly bitch.'

'Anyway, the bear who went to town is called Jonquil Charmwood and she lives at number four Powdermill Lane in Oakbridge. She's there now with the Reverend Lawrence.'

'I'm on my way,' Tennant said angrily. He turned to Potter. 'Sorry, Potter. I know you were wanting to get home.'

The inspector felt rather than saw his sergeant grow warm. 'Actually I had a date to play floodlit tennis tonight. I'd better ring and cancel.'

'Shame. Mixed doubles, was it?'

'Yes,' Potter answered enigmatically. 'It was.'

'Ah,' said Tennant, and relapsed into silence.

They reached Powdermill Lane thirty minutes later, Potter driving at top speed, to find the front door opened by the vicar. He held out his hand.

'Good evening, Inspector. I'm sure that this is the last thing you wanted but I honestly felt you ought to know.'

Thankfully Jonquil had regained her composure and having dived into the bathroom for ten minutes had more or less restored her face. She offered Tennant a glass of wine which he accepted with alacrity, Potter as usual had a cup of coffee. Glancing at Nick, Tennant thought he was somewhat the worse for wear but said nothing, thinking that the poor fellow was probably suffering with a bad case of wrung withers. He turned to look at Jonquil.

'Now tell me the story from the start,' he said, which she proceeded to do. Potter wearily got out his notebook.

When she had finished Tennant asked, 'And this girl, Emma Simms, you say is a friend of yours?'

'I don't know her all that well. In fact she's always struck me as rather a pathetic person. She's been in love for years with a married man who treats her like dirt and is quite happy about the situation. Anyway, I thought I would get her interested in the Odds and that's how she came to play the bear. To see if she liked the people. I smuggled her into the dress rehearsal – an earlier one. I thought she would pick up what she had to do from that.' Jonquil's lower lip trembled. 'I feel terrible now. Suppose something awful has happened to her.'

Tennant looked at his watch. 'It's just gone nine. I think it's a bit late to go calling on her flatmate. Give me her contact details and we'll get to her first thing in the morning. Thank you very much for the information, Miss Charmwood. I suggest you have a good night's sleep. I've always wanted to say 'Come along, Vicar' and now I'm going to get my wish. Come along, Nick, we'll give you a lift home. I somehow feel you'd fail the breath-alyser tonight.'

Jonquil looked contrite. 'Oh, you poor thing. We haven't had anything to eat yet.'

'Oh, never mind,' said Nick cheerfully. 'I can have a cheese sandwich when I get back.'

'Must you go?'

'I really think I should. I'll come and fetch the car in the morning.'

'It's up to you, Vicar,' said Tennant, quite seriously. 'You can stay with Miss Charmwood by all means.'

'Well, I think I'll take you up on your kind offer,' said Nick rather hastily. 'I have had quite a fair amount to drink this evening.' On the doorstep, he turned to the inspector. 'I kept sipping that wretched champagne while Jonquil was weaving her tale.'

'A strange story,' said Tennant reflectively.

'Very,' Nick answered sombrely.

They got into the car and he looked at the two policemen's heads from his seat in the back and wondered what they were thinking. It seemed odd to him that an unofficial understudy should go missing on the same night that Gerry Harlington had been thrown over the battlements. Was there a serial killer on the loose again? He said a silent and heartfelt prayer that the answer was no, remembering the horror and bloodshed of his previous encounter with such a creature. Yet he could see no thread linking a rather shy girl helping out a friend and an American hip-hop dancer turned movie actor. In fact there was none.

Nick shook himself. Emma Simms had probably gone off suddenly to see her mother and not left anyone a note. That was the most likely explanation. Or, perhaps, her married boyfriend had had some time to spare and had taken her away for a naughty few days. That was the most probable explanation of them all. The vicar sighed and fell asleep in the back of the police car.

SIXTEEN

T he Oakhurst Dramatists and Dramatic Society was in an emergency committee meeting. Paul Silas, fittingly clad in black trousers and a dark polo neck looked sombrely round the foregathered company and nodded his head in silence. He resembled Macbeth about to launch into his *Tomorrow and tomorrow and tomorrow* speech. So much so that Annette Muffat, the large blonde, had to control an unseemly fit of the giggles. But the rest of the members, particularly Mike and Meg Alexander, who were dying to take over the entire society, glared round them with cold, snake-like eyes.

Barry Beardsley spoke up. 'Well I know you got us here because of the present situation, Paul. But what particular aspect do you want us to consider?'

'The funeral, old boy,' came the answer in sepulchral tones.

'Have the police released the body?' asked Estelle Yeoman, the ex-professional.

'It is the coroner who does that. Not the police,' said Mike Alexander snappishly.

'All right, all right. Whoever. Has the body been released?'

'Not yet. But the day draws nearer I believe.' Paul sighed heavily. 'I shall go representing the Odds. Who will join me?'

Several people put up their hands, including Robin Green who announced, 'I have been interviewed by the police several times. I think they regarded me as prime suspect. But I believe I have finally got the message through to them that there were two different people involved and that I was neither of them.' He laughed, puffing an odour of milky tea into the atmosphere.

'What do you mean, two?' asked Barry Beardsley, who had had a simply dreadful day digging out corns and was in no mood to be trifled with.

'I've already told you a dozen times,' answered Robin. 'Somebody poked my legs with a stick which caused me to lose balance. While I was blinded by the helmet I heard the door to the other spiral staircase open and somebody made a sound—'

'That was our black friend,' interrupted Mike.

'It was an exhalation, just like when you push someone. Anyway I've told this to the police over and over again. They must have taken note of it by now.'

Cynthia Wensby, plain as a trodden-on sultana but an excellent treasurer for all her want of looks and talent, said eagerly, 'They've been to see me – twice.'

'They have been to see us all, my dear Cynthia,' said Paul in a bored-to-death voice. 'I had a charming little lady come round. Delightful wee creature – quite ravishing in fact. All violet eyes and smiles. We struck up quite a rapport.' He looked roguish.

'I tell you something,' said Annette Muffat into the sudden hush that followed. 'There was something funny about the bear the night of the show.' She turned to Jonquil Charmwood. 'Did you have a date, my dear, that you arrived so early and left before the end?'

Jonquil, who so far had not said a word to the meeting – something most unusual for her – went a nasty shade of plum but remained silent.

Meg Alexander, keen as a whippet scenting a hare, said, 'Hope he was worth it, my dear. It put the rest of us out considerably.'

'Yes, I had to dance the Charleston on my own,' Cynthia piped up, looking pained.

'You always dance on your own,' said somebody nastily.

Jonquil cleared her throat. 'I may as well tell the truth. I've told the police everything so I've nothing to hide. It wasn't me. I was given tickets for *Les Mis* and I went to see the show. I got someone else to understudy for me. Her name was Emma Simms and now the horrible thing is that she has vanished.'

There was a profound silence broken by Paul speaking as if he were sounding the death knell.

'What exactly do you mean by that?'

'What I just said. She disappeared four nights ago. She hasn't been seen since the Son et Lumière.'

'How very peculiar,' said Estelle. 'Are the police making enquiries?'

Silently, Jonquil started to cry. 'They've been to see her mother in the Isle of Man. I believe they've even been to question her boyfriend – which must have shocked the miserable bugger. They have looked everywhere but they can't find her. I think they are turning it into a murder enquiry.'

There was another protracted silence broken by Robin Green saying, 'The two things have got to be related. Perhaps your friend Emma saw something. Perhaps she saw the person who hit me on the legs – and she had to be silenced.'

'What rubbish you talk! How could witnessing someone playing a practical joke on you lead to the poor girl being murdered?'

'But she probably did see something,' put in Barry, and his tone was serious. 'Remember she hadn't been rehearsed properly and didn't know the lie of the land. She probably wandered about a bit, then I think the poor creature must have witnessed something happen and paid for it with her life.'

Now there was total silence from the committee broken only by the sound of Jonquil, who had put her arms down on the table and was weeping bitter tears of guilt.

*   *   *

Tennant was feeling depressed as he nearly always did when a case came up against an apparent dead end. Furthermore he had received the analysis of the substance beneath Gerry Harlington's eyes and been told it was salt water – tears. The fact that the black man had died slowly, weeping, and in enormous pain was too much even to contemplate. One wouldn't wish it on one's worst enemy. And now to muddy the waters entirely had come the strange disappearance of Emma Simms, as clean-living a girl as one could have hoped to meet providing that one overlooked her affair with Mr Garth Thorney, managing director of a small manufacturing company and the biggest bullshitter alive, at least in Tennant's opinion.

He had given Potter so much grief on the telephone that the inspector had intervened and called Mr Thorney into Lewes to make a statement about his relationship with Miss Simms. This had caused some blustering and the eventual threatening of Tennant with dire consequences because Mr Thorney played golf with his superior officer. But for all that he had agreed to report to police headquarters tomorrow morning. Another thing to add to Tennant's feeling of total despondency.

He got up from his chair and poured himself a large vodka and grapefruit juice, which he proceeded to sip thoughtfully. He and Potter had now come to the conclusion that the girl had either been abducted or killed, and Tennant felt almost certain that somehow or other it was connected with the Son et Lumière. But how? Unless she was making some sort of statement to the gallant Garth Thorney what could possibly be the purpose in vanishing? No, the coincidence of Emma taking part in the show in which the Wasp Man had met his death was far too great to be ignored.

Tennant crossed to the CD player and put on Olivia Beauchamp playing the Mendelssohn Violin Concerto. Then he sat down again and stared into space, wishing that he had not given up smoking but determined to stick with it. The sound of the music invaded his consciousness, blocking out all other thoughts – even a cigarette. When she played it was as if pearl drops formed, each droplet containing the most exquisite note that a human being could create. Tennant found that the tears were rolling down his cheeks at the pure ethereal beauty of what he was listening to. He wondered what instrument she had – surely it must be a Stradivarius – and made a mental note to ask her. He had a blinding flash of them standing together in the sunset, perhaps in Venice where all the world loved music, and she slowly raising the violin to her cheek and the glory of the sound she was creating reverberating and re-echoing past the ancient palaces, down the green waterway of the Grand Canal and out into the great lagoon that lay beyond. Sobbing like a fool, but quite unable to help himself, Tennant poured another vodka and headed for his bed.

SEVENTEEN

It was early evening and Rufus Beaudegrave was relaxing with a book in the Victorian sitting room. It was a week to the night of the single, fateful performance of the Son et Lumière and though he knew better than most that the police had their job to do he could not help but fret that people were still not allowed in to the castle. Because this was his income – or a least a major part of it – and he relied heavily on outside events to keep everything going. He was well aware that the bloodthirsty public would come rolling in as soon as the police cordon was removed but space was limited and he could only hope that the interest would persist for some time to come. The only good thing he had noticed was that balloon flights over the castle had increased, with people hanging over the side of the basket and pointing out the battlements and the place where they presumed the body had fallen. But to add to Rufus's general irritation was the fact that the press corps had set up camp in the fields on the far side of the moat. Whenever the family went out in the car they took photographs of him, his girls, even the old dog and despite polite requests for them to move on they weren't having any of it.

Rufus laid down his book and went to one of the windows which swept down to the floor, with shutters set in recesses beside them. Here he could look out over the moat, see it turning from blue to cobalt as the glow slowly drained from the day. His eyes took in the dim lights of the press people, some of whom had actually brought tents, whilst other less hardy souls had taken over all the nearby hostelries. But, as ever, his eyes were drawn to the starkly beautiful outlines of the castle, rearing majestically up against a sky in which the planet Venus was scintillating. And then his attention was drawn to something far nearer at hand. Floating in the water, a yard or two from the window at which he was standing, was a figure. Rufus was so startled that he pressed forward, leaning on the glass.

It looked for all the world like Millais' *Ophelia*. In the darkening day he could make out that it was female by the mass of wet fair hair floating round the deathly white face. He watched in horrible fascination as she drifted gently past him, one pale hand sticking up out of the water as if in supplication. Ophelia, for that was surely who it was, wore a billowing cloak that seemed to be keeping her afloat but beneath Rufus could see she had on another garment, which clung tightly to her body. A small wave broke around her and for a moment he looked directly into hollow terrible eyes before he let out a cry and took a step away. Then he watched in silent horror as, mermaid-like, she languorously glided out of his sight. Turning, he saw that his daughter Araminta had come silently into the room and was standing at the window next to his. She ran to him, her eyes horror-stricken.

'Oh, Daddy,' she said in a tiny voice that did not sound like hers at all. 'What was that?'

Rufus shook himself, literally, and regained control. 'I don't know, darling, but I shall phone the police and ask them to come.'

He walked to his armchair, which had a telephone standing beside it, dialled a number, then put out his other arm to cuddle Araminta, who suddenly seemed so small and vulnerable. A voice spoke at the other end and he answered, 'This is Rufus Beaudegrave of Fulke Castle speaking. I think you had better send some people over. I've just seen a body floating in my moat. I think perhaps a police diver might be a good idea.'

In the crook of his arm Araminta began to sob quietly.

'When is it all going to stop, Daddy?'

'When they catch the wicked person who is doing these things.'

'I do hope they hurry up.'

'So do I, my darling. So do I.'

*   *   *

It was one of the most bizarre scenes that Rufus had ever witnessed. Standing at the windows of the Tudor banqueting hall – the windows that looked out over the moat – he saw the police working by the floodlights that were switched on every night to light that great circle of water which held the castle safe in its nestling arm. The police had brought a boat and the diver had gone in and guided the body towards the shore. They had landed her just below where Rufus stood silently, gazing down at the horror unfolding beneath him. Just as soon as the body was landbound, two police photographers had stepped forward and had photographed the corpse from every conceivable angle, their cameras flashing in the darkness. Rufus knew that this was to catch it before it bloated up horrendously, distorting it beyond recognition. He had a glimpse of the face in the sudden flash of one of the cameras and saw that the eyes had glazed over and seemed to glare at him through their veils of blindness. Rufus's stomach heaved and he suddenly felt the loneliness of a single adult without a partner to share the whole ghastly business. His thoughts went to Ekaterina and he admitted at that moment that he wanted her badly. In every way. But the laws of good behaviour – in which he had been schooled constantly by his upright mama – forbade any such ideas. Nonetheless, Rufus walked through the silent and echoing castle to the nearest telephone.

By the time Tennant arrived on the scene the body was beginning to swell up, distorting the features of the face into a ghastly grin. He and Potter went into the tent that had been hastily erected. Stretched out on a table were the swollen remains of what had once been a young woman.

'Any identification on her?' he asked.

'None, sir. Except that she seemed to be wearing some sort of fancy dress. A black cloak of some description. Then the killer weighted her down with a saddle.'

Potter turned to his boss. 'Emma Simms, sir?'

'Probably. But we mustn't jump to any conclusions. Ah, here comes the doctor now.'

It was not the fresh-faced Cornish girl but a deputy who on this occasion turned out to be Dr Kasper Rudniski, aglow with

the honour of being on official police business. He greeted
Inspector Tennant with an enthusiastic shake of the hand.

'My dear Inspector, such a pleasure to see you again.'

'And to see you. But in rather grim circumstances I'm afraid.'

'Yes, indeed,' Kasper answered, looking serious.

He was very professional about his approach, examining the
swollen body with care and not removing the horse's saddle
which had weighted her down until Tennant had given his permission for it to be taken away. Eventually he raised his head.

'She either hit something in the water or somebody inflicted
a wound and then tied her down.'

'Which do you think?'

'The latter. I imagine her killer knocked her out then tied the
saddle on her by means of knotting the stirrups together.'

'Do you mean she was thrown into the water alive?'

'I think so. But the post-mortem will reveal the answers.'

'I presume it was the natural gases internally that brought her
to the surface again.'

'Correct. As her organs broke down they would have given
rise to gases which would make her come up from the depths
once more.'

'*Of his bones are coral made,*' quoted Tennant mystically.

Kasper looked a little puzzled but said nothing and Potter
contented himself with a quizzical glance at the doctor.

'Do you think this is the missing girl?' Kasper asked.

'I should think it highly likely. How long would you say she's
been in the water?'

'Several days.'

'Thank you. And thanks for your help, Dr Rudniski. I feel we
have rather put you on the spot.'

'It has been my pleasure, Inspector. My first experience of
police work.'

Potter thought to himself that people got satisfaction from the
most extraordinary things.

'It has taken me away from my day-to-day routine,' Kasper
continued. 'You know I was present when Gerry Harlington fell
to his death.'

'You actually witnessed the moment?'

'Yes.'

'And what did you think?'

'I thought it was the real thing. I even thought I heard a gasp on impact but the tape was playing so loudly that I realized I must be mistaken. I wish now that I had relied on my instincts.'

'Could you have saved him?'

'I doubt it. I think he would have died in hospital.'

'Yes, you're right of course. But do you know he wept as he lay dying. Poor bugger.'

Kasper looked grim. 'As you say, Inspector. He died a savage and cruel death.'

Rufus was sitting in his study having a scotch to calm his nerves before retiring for the night when there came a tap on the door. He called out 'Come in', and was surprised when Inspector Tennant appeared in the doorway.

Rufus stood up. 'My dear Inspector, what a terrible business. Do come in. Would you like a drink?'

Tennant glanced at his watch. It was a quarter to eleven. Potter was downstairs talking to uniform and the sergeant was driving.

'I'll join you in a scotch please, Sir Rufus.'

The two men sat down opposite each other and Rufus asked the inevitable question. 'Is this the girl who's gone missing?'

Tennant shook his head. 'I honestly don't know but my hunch is that it is.'

'I suppose she saw something at the Son et Lumière and had to be silenced.'

'I imagine so. But the point is, Sir Rufus, that there were either two people working together or a coincidence which gave the killer his – or her – advantage.'

'What do you mean exactly?'

'Well, the fall to the ground that preceded the heave over the battlements was no accident. Robin Green swears that someone came up the spiral stairs behind him and knocked him in the legs with a stick. And the killer – who must have been waiting on the spiral opposite – seized the opportunity and rushed at his victim and chucked him over the edge.'

Rufus stared into the dying flames. 'That is if Green is telling the truth.'

'Yes, that's occurred to us as well.' Tennant finished his drink and stood up. 'Thanks for seeing me. I'll leave you in peace. But I'm afraid the castle will remain out of bounds for the moment.'

'That's perfectly understandable. Let me escort you out.'

They walked together through the room that acted as an enclosed bridge, feeling the moat lapping at the arches beneath their feet.

'Do you ever get frightened here on your own?' Tennant asked.

Rufus gave a wry grin. 'I'm not on my own. I have four daughters and a handful of servants to keep me company.'

'Yes, of course. I don't know what I'm talking about. Forgive me.'

'You are perhaps referring to the fact that there is no woman in my life.'

'I suppose I was in a way.'

Rufus smiled. 'I hope to rectify that situation one of these days.'

Tennant turned to look at him. 'I hope very much that you do. Goodnight, sir.'

And the policeman walked out to his car wondering how he and the rest of the team were going to dodge the array of photographers waiting eagerly on the far side of the moat.

Nick was up early and was showered and shaved by eight o'clock in the morning. Pouring himself a bowl of muesli and sticking a couple of slices of bread in the toaster, he picked up a copy of the *Guardian* and, turning over the pages, was horrified to read a story headlined *Mystery of the Castle Deepens*. He read it quickly, then re-read it at a proper pace, digesting the facts while the toaster popped up his toast and let it slowly grow cold.

It seemed that yesterday evening the body of a young woman had been discovered in the moat at Fulke Castle. Though she had not yet been identified rumour was running high that it was the missing Emma Simms who had appeared in the performance of Son et Lumière during which Gerry Harlington, known to children throughout the world as the Wasp Man, had plunged to his death. The police had been called and Inspector Tennant of the Sussex Police had made a short statement, 'I have no comment to make at this time.' The story was accompanied by a tasteful photograph of Fulke Castle taken from the newspaper library. Unable to help himself Nick bolted from the vicarage to the newsagent opposite and bought a copy of *The Sun*. This was having a field day.

Wasp Man Second Death Mystery, ran the headline. *Last night a second corpse was found floating in the moat of Fulke Castle, the doomed and haunted building where only a week ago the body of famous film star Gerry (Wasp Man) Harlington was callously thrown over the battlements during a performance in which he was starring. The Sussex Police are baffled by that apparently motiveless crime. But now a second corpse was found to add to their problems.*

'It was, like, just floating past,' said Kimberley Dunne, assistant housekeeper. 'I thought it was a log but it seemed to have a kind of face. I was scared out of my wits.'

The body was that of an unknown woman but rumour is current that it is the remains of Emma Simms, a young actress also taking part in the same ill-fated show in which Gerry Harlington appeared. The castle is owned by Sir Rufus Beaudegrave who lives there with his four daughters. His wife ran off with a local gamekeeper some years ago and there has been no one in his life since. He refused to make any comment last night.

There were some blurred photographs of Dominic Tennant leaving the premises with a grim-faced Potter at the wheel of the car. This was accompanied by a photograph of the castle, deliberately darkened down to make it look frightening, and a huge picture of Gerry Harlington in full Wasp Man gear.

Nick sighed and laid down the paper and at that moment the telephone rang. He picked it up.

'Hello, Lakehurst Vicarage.'

'Is that you, Nick?' said a subdued female voice that he barely recognized.

'Jonquil?'

'Yes, it's me. Have you read the papers this morning?'

'Indeed I have.'

'The police have been on and want me to identify the body in the morgue.' She gulped.

'Why you? Hadn't Emma Simms got any other relatives? That is, if it is her.'

'Apparently not. She was an only child and her father is dead, while her mother lives on the Isle of Man – or somewhere equally remote. Nick, I'm terrified. I've never been to a mortuary. I'm afraid I might burst into tears or do something equally stupid.'

'When do you have to go?'

'This morning. They are very keen to get the identification done. I have to be at the mortuary in Lewes by eleven o'clock. A police car is coming to pick me up at ten.'

Nick said, 'Oh my dear, I would offer to go with you but this morning is absolutely impossible. I've got parish visits to the elderly and many of the old dears are housebound. They quite look forward to my coming. Say it brightens up their day.'

'Of course. I quite understand,' Jonquil answered in a voice that meant she did but couldn't help but resent it.

'Why not come and have supper with me tonight?'

Her tone brightened. 'Oh, could I really?'

'Of course. I feel I owe you a meal after our last slightly intoxicated meeting.'

'That was all the fault of that wretched policeman.'

'Tennant? No, trust me, Jonquil, he's a good bloke. Honestly.'

'I hope you're right, Nick. So what time shall I come?'

'About seven o'clock.'

'I'll be there, pale but determined.'

And what, thought Nick, as he hung up the phone, exactly was it that Jonquil was determined about?

EIGHTEEN

After the identification had been done; after a weeping Jonquil Charmwood had been taken into a side room and offered tea and biscuits; after Tennant and Potter had faced the grim reality that the bloated body lying in the morgue was indeed the mortal shell of Emma Simms, they had gone into conference back at Lewes Headquarters.

'Right, Potter, we're going to catch him – or her – and fast, before they decide to pick on somebody else.'

'I doubt that, sir.'

'What do you mean?'

'I doubt that it's a serial killer. It's pretty obvious to me that Emma saw something – wandering about as she was, not sure of the drill – and had to be got rid of.'

'That would be the obvious conclusion but one can never be sure of anything in a murder case,' Tennant answered pompously.

'Yes, sir. I learnt that many years ago.'

Tennant sighed. 'Sorry, I was trying to be a smart arse, a position which, when adopted, needs a sharp kick up same. Thanks for that.'

Potter grinned. He was, at last, growing more confident, more into his stride. Despite earlier reservations, Tennant was now convinced that he had a great future in the police force. The inspector shuffled the papers on his desk.

'These are the statements from every member of the cast and backstage crew regarding the night of the murder. I've read them all and there are several people that I want to interview again, including all the committee and the man who moved the body. Oh, and young Oswald as well.'

'Right, sir. When do we start?'

Tennant glanced at his watch. 'After lunch. We can see some of them at work, the others at home this evening.'

'What about Oswald? He seemed most unhappy when we interviewed him at his college.'

'Yes, you're right. We'll catch him in his lair this time.'

Tennant picked up the statements again. 'All right, Potter. I'll meet you outside at one thirty.'

Potter sloped off and Tennant stared at the pieces of paper again and again, realizing as he did so that nobody had asked any specific questions about the movements of the bear on the first night. It was of paramount importance to discover exactly what the ill-fated Miss Simms had done with herself before and after the Elizabethan Fair. Putting the statements to one side, Tennant stood up and allowed himself a few minutes to think, staring out of the window as he did so.

*   *   *

Punctually at half past one he and Potter took off towards Oakbridge. They had arranged their calls geographically and thus started with Estelle Yeoman, the ex-professional actress. They found her at home, dramatically dressed in a long scarlet skirt and black sweater, a purple scarf hung nonchalantly around her neck. She opened the front door and pulled a bit of a face on seeing the identity of her callers.

'Oh, hello. I didn't expect to see you again.'

'May we come in?' asked Tennant pleasantly.

'By all means,' she answered, and opened the front door wide.

Tennant, Potter following, notebook in hand, stepped into a hall laden with posters of various theatrical productions, including one from Tedmouth Repertory Company starring Estelle Yeoman as Marguerite in the stage version of *The Scarlet Pimpernel*. Tennant, frustrated thespian that he was, stood staring at them, thinking that the venues were somewhat second rate. Estelle, however, misunderstood and stood smiling at him beatifically.

'Those were the days,' she said. 'You interested in the theatre, Inspector?'

'Oh yes, I enjoy a good show,' he answered, knowing that at one time it had been his burning desire to become a professional actor and how nowadays he no longer had the time or energy to do anything but the smallest character role.

Estelle nodded and called up the stairs, 'Fizz dear, we've got company. It's the police. Make us some coffee, there's a love.' She smiled at Tennant. 'I presume you won't have anything stronger?'

'Thank you, no. On duty and all that.'

They followed her into an audacious sitting room, the walls painted deepest red with a large picture of a female nude lying provocatively on a bed hanging over the fireplace.

Estelle turned to them. 'Do sit down and tell me how I can help you.'

'Well,' Tennant answered, thinking how attractive she was, 'did you notice anything unusual at the one and only performance of Son et Lumière? Was there anybody out of place? Or anything, come to that?'

She frowned. 'I thought it odd that Robin – he was playing one of the knights – fell over backwards. I was watching from the side by the way. The choreography of the fight had gone out of the window and now we all know why. But from where I was standing I could swear that at that moment the door leading to the staircase behind Gerry Harlington swung open a fraction, though it was pretty dark up there.'

'Did you see anybody come out of the door?'

'No, that's the bugger of it. I didn't see a soul. And the next second Gerry took the famous tumble and crashed to the earth below.'

'Very realistically,' said Tennant drily.

'Indeed,' Estelle answered, looking thoughtful.

There was a moment's silence then Tennant said, 'I'd like to turn to the subject of the bear if I may. You know that Emma Simms took the part that night.'

'Yes, and she's gone missing. It's been all over the papers.'

'Then you have probably read about the body in the moat.' Estelle nodded. 'Well, I have to tell you that it has been identified.'

Estelle looked stricken. 'Emma?'

'I'm afraid so.'

The door opened at that moment and Estelle said, 'Oh, this is my partner, Fizz.'

Tennant and Potter looked up and saw a wildly pretty girl staggering beneath a large tray laden with cups, saucers, a cafetière and a mass of homemade biscuits, judging by their fresh oven smell.

'Thanks, darling,' said Estelle casually.

Tennant rose to his feet and asked if he could help but Fizz waved him aside and lurched towards a coffee table and thankfully placed the tray upon it. She looked towards the inspector with a beautiful smile.

'Thought you might like a homemade biscuit,' she said in a little-girl voice.

Potter took one and shot his boss a somewhat amused grin. Tennant pretended he hadn't seen it.

'Fizz and I met in rep,' Estelle continued in a matter-of-fact manner. 'She's resting at the moment but there's a TV producer hot on her heels. Isn't he, love?'

'Yes,' lisped Fizz.

'Well done,' said Tennant with not a flicker of a smile. 'But if you don't mind, Miss Yeoman, I've come to talk about Miss

Simms. Now, cast your mind back, did you notice anything odd about the bear on the night of the performance?'

'Well, yes and no. First of all she was already in costume when I arrived which I thought odd. But no doubt you've heard all this already. But then I think she must have changed some- where because I thought I saw a strange girl wandering about.'

'Would it be this girl?' interrupted Potter promptly, and produced a photograph of the body taken as soon as it had come out of the water.

Fizz let out an endearing little scream and Estelle patted her hand fondly.

'I'm not sure. This is rather ghoulish, isn't it?'

Potter looked straight faced. 'I'm sorry if it upsets you, madam, but we have to photograph a victim of drowning as soon as they come out of the water. After that the body swells up and is almost unrecognizable.'

'Well, it could be but I wouldn't swear to it.'

Tennant nodded. 'If you could just tell me where you saw the girl and what she was doing.'

'Just that. Wandering. She was wearing a green dress with a rather fetching scarf round her neck. I would have challenged her but I didn't have time. I was just about to go on as the twen- ties Lady Beaudegrave. And that scene was all mucked up because Jonquil wasn't there. She was supposed to do the Charleston with Barry but as she didn't appear he grabbed me instead.' She grinned. 'But that's show business for you.'

'Indeed it is.'

Tennant stood up. 'Thank you for your help, Miss Yeoman. If you should think of anything else regarding the strange girl or Mr Harlington please don't hesitate to ring me.'

He handed her his card. She tucked it into a pocket of her skirt.

'There's one thing, Inspector.'

'Yes?'

'Gerry Harlington was a complete prat and though he didn't deserve the ending he got the theatre is better off without him.'

'Thank you for your views,' said Tennant solemnly, and allowed Fizz to show him and Potter out.

* * *

Their next call was on Annette Muffat who was quite scary close to, reminding the inspector of a drag queen. Her blonde Farah Fawcett hair was dark as a starless midnight at the roots and her slightly orange make-up was caked in the little lines around her eyes. Her lipstick was deepest crimson and did not suit her, nor did her outfit, which consisted of a pair of black leggings with a puce tunic over the top. She was at work in a healthy baker's shop when the pair of policemen called and her smile of welcome turned to an icy stare when she saw who had just pinged the bell.

Tennant produced his badge with a flourish and introduced Potter, then said, 'Can we step into the back, please. We would like to speak to you in private.'

Annette clicked her tongue against her teeth and said, 'Oh really! Can't you see I'm on my own.'

Potter answered, 'Then we can speak in here.'

She looked grumpy. 'Well, what is it?'

'As you can probably guess,' said Tennant equably, 'it's about the murder of Gerry Harlington. Did you see anything unusual that night? Anything at all? Anybody out of place, for example?'

'Well, hardly. I was in the bloody changing tent when it happened. Getting ready for the Elizabethan Fair scene. But I've already told the police all this.'

'Forgive me,' Tennant answered, turning on the pixieish charm. 'I know what a bore it must be for you – going over old ground like this. But we poor coppers like it spelled out, I'm afraid. Tell me, was the bear in the tent with you?'

Annette paused and stared at the inspector, being rewarded with a warm gooseberry gaze which quite unsettled her.

'Now you come to mention it, I don't think she was.' She looked into space. 'No, I'm sure she wasn't.'

'Have you any idea where she was?'

'No, unless she was in the toilet.'

'That would have been a bit awkward wouldn't it. In her bear skin and all,' put in Potter.

'If she'd had any sense she would have gone before she changed,' answered Annette forthrightly. 'But now we know that dear little Jonquil fielded a stand-in. I don't suppose the poor kid would have known her way around at all.'

'You do realize that it was Emma Simms, the missing girl?' asked Tennant.

Annette sat down heavily. 'Oh my God. I hadn't made the connection. So she's been found.'

'Alas, yes.'

Annette was silent for a few minutes. 'I see it all now. Jonquil didn't brief her properly and she was told just to put on her bear skin and do a little dance. That's all the poor girl knew.'

Tennant nodded in silent agreement, then said, 'I take it you don't like Jonquil Charmwood very much.'

'I can't stand the stuck-up little bitch. Flounces into rehearsals all blonde hair and long eyelashes. Thinks all the men are in love with her, which they probably are, stupid gits.'

The inspector, thinking of the poor sobbing creature whom he had escorted into the morgue that morning could hardly agree with the description, then thought how tragedy changed people, and hoped the bouncy Miss Charmwood would not be altered forever by her recent experience. An experience as stark as the one she had just had could well mar her for life.

He smiled at Annette. 'I think you will find her somewhat different. She was asked to identify Miss Simms's body this morning and has been terribly shaken by the whole affair.'

Miss Muffat looked as if she would like to say 'Serve the silly cow right' but instead said, 'Oh dear.'

Potter cleared his throat. 'Can you think of any connection between Gerry Harlington and Miss Simms, Miss Muffat?'

'None, except, of course, that they both met in the darkness the same murderer.'

NINETEEN

This morning Ricardo drove with purpose to his massage appointment, determined to get Ekaterina into a better frame of mind.

To his surprise she came running out of the door as soon as

he arrived, looking spectacular in a pair of Ginger Rogers trousers and a loose sweater, created, of course, by Jean Paul Gaultier.

'Ricardo, please do me a big favour,' she said by way of greeting.

'Of course, madam,' he answered, bowing as he got out of the car and banging his head as a result.

'I want you to take me to Fulke Castle,' she said surprisingly.

Ricardo could have fainted with shock. 'Fulke Castle?' he repeated slowly.

'Yes. I had a phone call from Sir Rufus asking if I would visit him and I think it only polite to do so.'

Ricardo couldn't help it; a rather stupid grin spread over his features.

'But there is a problem,' Ekaterina continued. 'The paparazzi are on the land side of the moat taking photographs and even more of them have arrived since the body has been discovered. Somehow I want you to smuggle me in.'

'You could lie on the back seat of my car and I could cover you with a blanket.'

'Yes, that is a good plan.'

'And I could put a box of oils and creams on top of you.' Ricardo was warming to his theme.

'Even better. We shall go immediately.'

'But I haven't got a blanket.'

'Then I will fetch one.'

She ran into the house again, then reappeared clutching a tartan picnic rug.

'I hope I will be able to breathe through this.'

'Well, you need only cover your face at the last minute.'

Ekaterina threw her arms round him spontaneously. 'You are so clever. Thank you for your help. I couldn't have managed without you.'

Ricardo helped her into the back seat of his car and arranged the rug over her, putting his box of goodies on her feet. Then they took off for the castle only to be stopped at the gatehouse by a guard built like a sumo wrestler, with a huge fist and face of mega proportions.

'Yes?' he said, waving Ricardo's car to a halt and thrusting his mighty mug in through the rolled down window.

'Massage for Sir Rufus,' said Ricardo in a very Italian accent.

'Oh yes? He didn't say nothing to me.'

'Ring him then. Say it is the masseur from Mrs Harlington.'

That did the trick and having made a brief call the guard waved them in. But Ricardo had not been quite clever enough. As Ekaterina removed the blanket from her face and laughed, a photographer who had managed to make his way on to the bridge suddenly reared up and snapped them, thinking it a bit of a coup. Ricardo's heart plummeted as Ekaterina let out a shriek.

'I think it would be best if Sir Rufus immediately put you on his visiting list,' he remarked.

'But I don't think he would believe that proper behaviour with me being so recently widowed.'

'It is not proper behaviour that makes the world go round,' Ricardo answered wisely.

Tennant was sitting in his office in Lewes looking at all the reports he had taken on the previous day. The four people he hadn't so far had time to see were Mike and Meg Alexander, Paul Silas and Oswald Souter. Looking through the statements carefully it seemed that several people had noticed the bear wandering about before the Elizabethan fair but nobody had had time to say anything to her.

'It was one mad rush getting into costume,' Barry Beardsley had said, still in his white coat from having seen an ingrown-toenail sufferer. 'I thought she looked a bit lost but I just put it down to Jonquil having a turn, if you know what I mean. Very unsettled in her love life, that young woman.'

'In what way?' Potter had asked.

'She's a terrible flirt is Jonquil. Has boys round her like the proverbial bees and honey pot. If she hasn't got six on the go she isn't happy.'

'Does she sleep with them all?'

'Not many, if rumour be true. But who am I to say? You will have to ask her that. If it's relevant to the enquiry.'

There had been a silence while Tennant had thought and in the end he had said, 'It might be. Thank you, Mr Beardsley.'

Now he wondered if any ex-boyfriend of Jonquil's had mistaken the wretched Emma for Miss Charmwood, heavily disguised as the bear as she had been. He thought it was worth a follow-up at least and decided to put Potter on to it. He was just about to pick up his phone when it rang.

A voice spoke. 'Hello, sir. It's James from forensics. Sorry we've taken so long with that bit of fur you found.'

'Did you get anything?'

'Well, we did a skin sample on the interior and found there was some evidence of the wearer. In other words we got some DNA from it.'

'And?'

'That's what caused the delay. We took some specimens from the body in the moat – Emma Simms – and it was her. She was the last person to wear that fur.'

'Christ, it was the bear skin!' Tennant shouted. 'That poor kid must have wandered up on to the battlements and actually witnessed the murder. By God, James, you deserve a drink for this.'

'I'll hold you to that, Inspector.'

Tennant hurried into the room where his team were busy at their computers.

'Listen, everybody,' he said loudly. 'The bit of fur on the battlements came from the bear skin that Emma Simms was wearing. Her DNA has been found on it. She must have gone up there to get a better view and seen the murderer – whoever he or she was. That's why she was killed.'

'Do you think she tripped up Robin Green, guv?'

'It's possible I suppose, though what possible motive she could have had I really can't imagine.'

'Perhaps he was an ex-boyfriend.' This from Morgana with the wood-violet eyes.

'You haven't seen him,' Tennant answered, and laughed hilariously.

'That bad huh?'

'That bad.'

Potter walked in and Tennant passed on the glad tidings.

'Then come on, sir. We've really got to find out who was wandering round on the battlements as well as that pathetic bear.'

'I suggest we have another look at them.'

'And the spiral staircases as well.'

'Let's go.'

*   *   *

They passed through the battery of pressmen and presented themselves at the gatehouse where the man built like a megalosaur duly waved them down.

'Police,' said Potter, flashing his badge.

'And the other one?' asked the guard, indicating Tennant with a jerk of his vast head.

'My inspector.'

'Pass on.'

'Where the hell did Sir Rufus find him?' Tennant asked as the car moved out of earshot.

'In a monastery somewhere?'

'Probably Brother Corpulentia.'

'Shouldn't that be Corpulentius?'

'Clever dick,' said Tennant and laughed at his own joke.

Having spoken to the housekeeper – Sir Rufus apparently being out for a ride – the two policemen made their way up the first spiral, the one that Robin Green must have climbed that night. But this time they went up each step carefully, looking at anything and everything. Tennant knew well that by now any forensic material would be well and truly corrupted but really the search was for his own benefit, anything that would give him a lead on the two burning questions. Firstly, who had been on the stairs that night, had opened the door above and poked Robin Green in the legs with a stick? Could it have been Emma Simms? But if so, why? The second question was who had crept up the staircase in the opposing tower and rushed at Gerry Harlington from the back? Many people had disliked the man but who had disliked him enough to kill him?

Potter reached the top of the spiral and stepped out on to the battlements. A fine view of the castle and the surrounding countryside lay before him but his mind was churning over other thoughts. He turned to Tennant.

'The odd thing is that Gerry Harlington could have had no idea that Adam Gillow was going to be delayed on the train that night. And how did he manage to get in here unobserved?'

'I think the answer is relatively simple. He had sworn revenge on Robin Green for trying to strangle him and I truly believe that he meant to kill him with the sword. We know from his films that he was used to swordplay and I am sure that was

his intention. I think that he got here early in the morning and
hid himself in the bushes which grow plentifully on the island.
Furthermore, I believe he went into that dressing tent long
before the cast had arrived and dressed himself as a knight.
As we all know, once the helmet is on it is impossible to
recognize anyone. His one stroke of good luck was that Adam
was delayed on the train.'

'But somebody must have seen him?'

'Yes, his murderer. He probably went up to the battlements
long before his scene and the killer spotted him and decided to
act. It was a spontaneous killing.'

'You're absolutely sure that the murderer didn't have a partner
working with him. Someone who deliberately tripped Green up
at just the right moment.'

The inspector sighed wearily. 'I've thought and thought about
it. Unless it was Emma herself, but I wouldn't have believed
she would have known what scene was coming when. In other
words I think the tripping up was done by someone fully
conversant with the show. But whether they were working with
the murderer I just don't know. And I feel a fool for not
knowing.'

They climbed the second staircase, which ran parallel to the
other, with equal care, looking for something fresh, something
other than the fountain pen that Tennant had found on the first
day. But there was nothing to see.

Once again but from the other angle they stepped out on to
the battlements. Tennant gazed out at the panorama before him.
And then his eye was caught by two distant horsemen riding
in the parkland that lay beyond the moat and away from the
direction in which the press men had their camp.

'Well, well,' he said. 'Hey, Potter, come and look at this.'

Potter, nervous of heights, edged to his side. 'It's Sir Rufus,
isn't it? But who's the woman with him?'

'None other than the merry widow herself.' Tennant laughed.
'I wonder if we've been barking up the wrong tree all along.'

'Good Lord, perhaps you're right. But they've both got cast-
iron alibis.'

'Which they gave each other.'

'Indeed they did.'

'*Cherchez la femme*, Potter. That's what my old mama used to say.'

'I think we should have another word with them, don't you?'

'I most certainly do,' answered Tennant.

TWENTY

It was late afternoon and Nick had stolen a few delightful moments in his autumnal garden, a vivid, sweet-smelling harmony of russet and ochre. On the trees the remaining leaves had crisped and dried into cockleshells. The flowers still bravely blooming in the beds were a combination of deepest scarlet and the soft gentle mauve of Michaelmas daisies. It seemed as though the earth itself was quietly going into the deep sleep of winter, as if everything was slowing down in preparation for the hardest months of the year.

The vicar breathed deeply, closed his eyes and let his mind wander off at a tangent. He thought about the vastness of the ever-expanding universe and how short a span mortals were given in it. He thought about the cruelties of murder and about the terrible way in which Gerry Harlington had met his end. Slowly and almost reluctantly his mind turned to God and Nick felt in that moment that the Almighty must be so vast and infinite that mankind must make the best of the situation without His help. Then he shook himself. It was not part of his training for the priesthood to harbour such thoughts. But still they came in the darkness of night to haunt him. Nick shook himself again, really hard this time, and turned to go into the house. Then the ringing of the doorbell penetrated his consciousness and with a great sense of relief he went to answer it.

Jonquil Charmwood stood there, ashen faced.

'Oh Nick,' she said, and flung herself weeping into his arms.

They stood there in full view of the High Street with Jonquil sobbing bitterly and deeply, the noise raking her throat and making her seem so vulnerable.

'Come in, come inside,' said Nick quietly, and all at once his faith in his mission in life returned to him and he felt strong enough to bear her sorrows.

She could not speak, could not say a word to him, but she let him draw her quietly into the kitchen where he sat her down on a wooden stool and, going to his bar, poured her a large shot of brandy.

'Jonquil, my dear, tell me what is the matter. I am here to help you, remember.'

She looked at him for the first time and Nick thought he had never seen such a change in anyone. Gone was the laughing, vivacious blonde who had called on him only a short while ago to ask his opinion of Gerry Harlington. In her place had come a caricature of the girl that once was. Her hair hung limply, her face was unmade up, her lips were pale and drawn.

'Oh Jonquil,' he said, and gave her a spontaneous hug.

She gazed up at him and he thought her eyes looked newly washed, brimming with tears that she had yet to shed.

'Oh Nick, it was so awful. That's why I couldn't come to supper last night. I couldn't have seen anyone. It was the sight of poor Emma lying there. The trouble was I hardly recognized her. And then came the realization that I had sent her to her death. That if it hadn't been for me and my stupid theatre trip she would be alive today.'

Nick, who was beginning to think that Jonquil was prone to weeping bitterly whenever she saw him said, 'Oh come now, that is hardly true, is it?'

'But it is. Think about it.'

And the vicar had to admit that what Jonquil had just said was undeniably a fact. Nevertheless he did his best to dissuade her.

'Look, Jonquil, people have been saying what you just said from time immemorial. Think about those on the Titanic. I'm sure the women in the lifeboats must have thought that as they gazed back at their stranded men.'

He was talking rubbish and he knew it, for what the mighty marine disaster could possibly have to do with a poor dead girl he could not possibly think. Jonquil, too, looked puzzled.

'Do you mean that they were all drowned?'

'Yes,' said the vicar, clutching at straws, 'that is exactly what I meant.'

Jonquil stared at him in tear-stained awe and finally let out a sob-laden giggle.

'What you're saying makes no sense.'

'No, I know it doesn't. But at least it made you stop crying.'

'Oh Nick,' she answered, and collapsed in his arms once more, but this time no longer weeping.

Tennant and Potter had thoroughly searched the battlements and the spiral staircases leading thereto and had come away empty handed. The trail to the killer had gone stone cold – not that it had ever been hot.

A car was drawing up as they were about to get into theirs and they paused a moment to see who was arriving at Fulke Castle. Out of the back seat came two little girls in school uniform, their blonde hair flying behind them, their little faces bright with the joy of living. On seeing the two policemen they hurried forward and introduced themselves.

'Hello, I am Ondine . . .'

'And I am Perdita . . .'

'Beaudegrave,' they finished together.

'Can we help you?' asked the older of the two, giving Tennant a marvellous smile.

With a glance at Potter he solemnly shook their respective hands.

'How do you do? I am Inspector Dominic Tennant and this is my Sergeant, Mark Potter.'

'Are you policemen?' asked the smaller one, Perdita.

'Yes, we are. Do we look different from other people?'

'No, not really. But you have an official air.'

Tennant cracked into a laugh. 'Really? You do surprise me. I always thought we blended in.'

Two pairs of eyes regarded him seriously. 'You do and you don't,' answered Ondine.

'You have beautiful names, the pair of you. Did your father choose them?'

'Actually Granny put in her twopenn'orth,' answered Perdita, and grinned at Potter, who grinned broadly back. 'I like you,' she continued. 'Will you come and have tea with us? It's only in the kitchen I'm afraid.'

'I think we ought to get your father's permission first,' said Tennant.

'Oh he's out riding with Mrs Harlington.' The two men exchanged a glance. 'That's why Tom fetched us from school.'

'I see. Well in that case we would be delighted to accept.'

'Oh goody,' said Perdita.

The children led them through the shadowy recesses of the castle's many rooms until they finally passed through a door and into a bright and cheerful kitchen. Big by anybody's standards, its amazing amount of copper utensils, obviously passed down in the family for a considerable length of time, gleamed where they hung on two huge dressers. A big pine table stood in the centre of the room, laid with a blue-and-white gingham cloth. Sir Rufus's housekeeper looked up in some surprise as the two policemen entered the room.

'Oh, good afternoon, gentlemen. I didn't realize you were coming to tea.'

'Miss Ondine and Miss Perdita invited us.'

'Does Sir Rufus know?'

'Oh, don't be stuffy, Miggy. Of course he does,' answered Ondine swiftly.

'Very well. I'll lay two more places.'

At this point the rest of Sir Rufus's brood came in; Araminta, black haired and beautiful, and Iolanthe, with hair like a fox's coat. Tennant could visualize them in the future, at parties, clutching a glass, laughing, the very centre of attention. The inspector suddenly envied Rufus and wished life had turned out differently for him.

'Aren't you both policemen?' asked Araminta pointedly.

'Yes they are and they are my guests,' answered Ondine, very hoity-toity.

Araminta shrugged. 'Whatever.'

Tennant broached the subject that interested him. 'Did any of you girls see the Son et Lumière?'

'Yes, we all did,' said Perdita, widening her doll eyes. 'We saw the dress rehearsal – and the night of the murder. We thought Gerry Harlington was an absolute prat.'

'Really? Why's that?' asked Potter, halfway through a sandwich.

'That ridiculous dance he did on the rehearsal night. Talk about out of place,' Araminta put in.

'Don't you like hip-hop?' asked Tennant innocently.

'I like it well enough but not done in the middle of an Elizabethan Fair scene. I mean, he came on looking as if he'd just come out of a dustbin and proceeded to cavort. I was told there was an awful punch-up at the end. Even the vicar was involved.' She giggled.

Tennant smiled. 'It sounds well deserved to me. Tell me, did you see all of the dress rehearsal?'

'Yes. Daddy was sitting in the audience but we went to the Tudor dining hall and looked out of the window.'

'And what about the performance? Did you see all of that as well?'

'Oh yes. This time we were officially in the dining hall. It was really very exciting to watch.'

'Did your father sit downstairs again?' asked Potter.

'No he was with us. And so was that beautiful Russian woman. Ekaterina.'

'I didn't realize they knew one another,' lied Tennant.

'Oh yes. They are quite friendly,' said Iolanthe, the afternoon sun filtering through one of the windows turning her foxfire hair molten.

There was a sudden silence, Tennant longing to ask if anyone had left the room for any length of time but not quite certain how to put it. He could feel Potter looking at him, then heard his sergeant clear his throat.

'Did anyone go out for anything?'

Araminta's voice was steely as she answered, 'If you mean did Daddy or Ekaterina leave the room for a while, the answer is no. Daddy went to get some more logs for the fire and was gone five minutes. Ekaterina went to the lavatory during the interval and I went with her because she didn't know where it was. So neither of them could have done the murder if that is what you wanted to know.'

'Yes,' Potter answered honestly, 'that is what I was asking. You see, Miss Beaudegrave, when somebody is killed one has to follow every lead, however hurtful it might be. I do hope you will accept my explanation.'

She turned on him a face which spoke of generations of good breeding.

'Of course. You are only doing your job. Would you like a piece of cake?'

'Yes please,' said Potter, and the moment passed.

Outside the two men looked at one another and as soon as the car had started began to talk.

'Well, that's that line of enquiry buttoned up. You did well, Potter. I was terrified to ask.'

'Thank you, sir. Nice girls, aren't they? Going to be stunners when they get older.'

'Indeed they are. Now we'll be just in time to join Mike and Meg Alexander who should be pouring out a glass of preprandial sherry. I can almost smell it from here. Let's go.'

And they drove out of the gatehouse and away in the direction of Oakhurst.

Jonquil had cheered up, that is to say that she was only crying once an hour as opposed to once every ten minutes. Nick, who had grown quite fond of her, was trying to talk her out of her conviction that she had sent Emma Simms to her death. Yet it was difficult, because it was more or less true. The vicar had considered musing about God's mysterious ways but had decided against it. Jonquil had the look of someone determined to wallow in despair. And yet, he thought, this mood could not possibly last for ever. Hidden deep within was a bubbly person who would insist on eventually returning. Jonquil was by nature a cheerful creature and no disaster, however daunting, would diminish that side of her character. So he let her maunder on until eventually she ran out of steam and put on some make-up and accepted his invitation to supper and decided to be as jolly as was possible in the circumstances.

Mike Alexander answered the door and regarded Tennant with a gimlet eye.

'Yes?' he said, in the voice that one might use to an unwanted canvasser.

The inspector flashed his badge at the same moment that Potter produced his. Neither of them had met Alexander before and they watched his features undergo a rapid change, adopting a hail-fellow-well-met expression.

'Ah ha,' he said cheerily. 'An Inspector Calls and all that. Did you see that marvellous production at the National? Many years ago now. Do you go to the theatre, Inspector?'

'Yes, whenever I get the time, I do. May we come in?'

'But of course. Certainly, certainly.'

He bowed them into a living room that Tennant felt shouted fussiness. There were bows everywhere – on the curtains, on the cushions, in the hair of a small dog that sat peevishly growling on the hearth rug. There was even a festoon of fake flowers and wheat cuttings adorned with a bow that hung on the outside of the door. The inspector, who was once more collecting Staffordshire pottery, looked with distaste at a cabinet full of crinolined ladies making moues and girls from the twenties with simpering faces.

Meg Alexander, who was sitting on the sofa with a glass of sherry in hand – Potter gave Tennant a surreptitious wink – was not at all what he had anticipated. Theatrical she might indeed be but she looked far more like a retriever-walking woman from the Home Counties. She was not fat but large, tall and big-boned, with a head of silver hair swept back in an old-fashioned pleat. She had ample feet, presently encased in a low-heeled pair of shoes in navy and white, and hands like a man. She looked up enquiringly as the two policemen entered the room.

'Inspector Tennant, darling,' called Mike jovially. 'And Sergeant Pitter.'

'Potter actually, sir.'

'Of course. How foolish of me. Gentlemen, take a seat. Can I get you a drink?'

'No, thank you. On duty and all that.'

'You won't mind if I have one?' Mike continued in the same merry tones. 'Steady the nerves before my grilling.' He laughed at his own joke and nobody joined in.

'I believe you saw one of my other officers,' said Tennant by way of an opening gambit.

'Oh yes, a delightful girl. Very lovely eyes.'

From the sofa Meg waved a large and languid hand. 'I didn't know they made police officers so pretty. Mike quite fell for her, didn't you sweetie?'

'I'm pleased to hear it,' answered Tennant, straight faced.

She gave him a sharp look but he smiled at her urbanely and said, 'I expect you're wondering why I am here as you have already been interviewed. The answer is that we are now making enquiries about the death of Emma Simms.'

'Yes, of course,' said Mike, foregoing the sherry and pouring himself a large scotch. 'The poor girl who played the part of the bear during Miss Charmwood's little theatre excursion.'

'That's the one,' put in Potter cheerfully.

Meg sat upright and looked Tennant directly in the face. He couldn't help but notice that her eyes were an odd colour, the kind of grey that his mother would have described as 'Walrus Whiskers'. They also had a coldness about them that he did not altogether trust.

'Sad little wretch,' she said, exuding a smell of Poison by Dior as she moved. 'That girl should never have gone off like that. I am referring to Miss Charmwood of course. That's the trouble with the Odds, they lack a true sense of theatrical responsibility. Mike and I were both members of the Tooting Bec Acting Society, you know. Now there was a drama group of which one could say one was proud to be a member. Not any old actor could join, in fact quite the reverse. There were strict auditions and when I say strict I am speaking of National Theatre standards. Mike, who was chairman, saw to that.'

A horrible picture was beginning to form in Tennant's mind of a stultified drama group, run by the Alexanders, who considered themselves God's gift to the stage and let everybody know it. They would have gathered round them a clique of yes-men and nobody else would have stood a chance of a part, particularly those with genuine talent.

'Did you ever play Lear?' was on his lips before he knew it.

Mike stood still, whisky glass in hand. 'Alas no,' he said sonorously. 'Of course it's my ambition to so do – who would not wish to take such a role? – but with the Odds there is no chance of it coming to pass. Or if it did that man of mediocrity, Paul Silas, would make sure he played the lead. It's a sad thing that we ever had to leave the Tooting crowd.'

'Why did you?' asked Potter, curious.

Mike gave a deep sigh and Meg answered for him.

'Change of job, alas. The company Mike was working for moved their headquarters to Milton Keynes and we didn't think that was quite . . .' She gave a little smile. 'Anyway, we decided to come to Sussex and we ended up in Oakbridge. But quite frankly, Inspector, the Odds are not to our liking. We are thinking of leaving and forming our own company, aren't we, darling?'

She leaned over and squeezed his hand and he gazed at her with apparent adoration.

'We want to play *Heloise and Abelard*, a two-hander,' she continued. 'Do you know it?'

'Yes,' Tennant answered shortly. His ex-wife and her lover had performed it and though he had not gone to see it, other friends had and told him it was glutinously cloying.

Tennant cleared his throat. 'As I was saying, we are here to enquire about the death of Emma Simms. So if you don't mind awfully I would like to ask you some questions.'

Mike joined Meg on the sofa where they sat closely side by side with identical expressions of avid interest. Tennant felt a wild desire to giggle, which he fought back manfully.

'I'm going to talk about the one and only night she was there. Now, just to fill me in completely can you tell me what scenes you were in and what you were doing when you were off stage, as it were.'

They both spoke together then Mike gave a deprecating little laugh and said, 'Ladies first.'

'I wasn't in the first scene, of course, that was Paul Silas, solo.' Her mouth tightened as she said this and Mike muttered, 'Naturally!'

Meg continued. 'The second scene was the building of the castle and I wafted on in medieval gear as the first Lady Beau De Grave, accompanied by Paul and most of the men as the builders.'

'Had you seen Miss Simms by this time?'

'Yes, she was in the dressing room when I arrived.'

'Yes, she was,' echoed Mike.

'And what happened after that?'

'Well, I had a long pause during the trouble with the See of Canterbury scene. I wandered about a bit in my Elizabethan costume and it was then that I saw Emma . . .'

Meg stopped short and her face flushed a dusky unbecoming red.

'Oh yes,' asked Tennant, 'and where would that have been?'

'I can't really remember.'

'I think you can, Mrs Alexander.'

'I believe it was going up the stairs leading to the battlements.'

'I see,' answered the inspector – and he did, a great deal. He felt rather than saw Potter stiffen beside him and he let his sergeant ask the next question.

'Was it you, Mrs Alexander, who climbed the spiral stairs and poked Robin Green in the back of the legs, causing him to fall down? And I warn you that to lie at this juncture could do a lot more harm than good. You have made it perfectly clear that you hated the Odds and wanted to form a separate company. Either that or to take them over completely. Wouldn't it have suited your purpose to make them look like a load of amateur halfwits? Which, no doubt, was in your mind when you gave Robin a hearty shove.'

Meg battled with herself, wondering what to do for the best, ignoring Mike's signals to keep quiet. Eventually she spoke with such patent dislike that Tennant was vividly reminded of Lady Macbeth and wondered if he was in the presence of a killer.

'Yes I did – and why not? I really resented Green being given that part. Mike should have done it. He's very fit – plays golf, squash, goes to the gym – he was ideal for the role. But no! It was Robin's turn to get a good part and so the little runt was given it. So I thought I would spoil his big moment for him. I went up the stairs and saw the bear standing on the battlements. The poor little soul must have wanted a better view or something. Anyway, I knocked Robin down and retreated fast.'

'Did you then go up the other stairs and push Gerry Harlington from behind?' asked Tennant in a calmly quiet voice.

'No, I didn't. I didn't know that he was there or I might have been tempted. You find the person who knew about the substitution and you will have got your murderer, Inspector.'

Even though he didn't want to, Tennant found himself both believing and agreeing with her. Nevertheless, she had committed an act of assault on Robin Green and would be charged accordingly.

'Potter, charge Mrs Alexander with assault will you.'

Meg snarled and it struck Tennant yet again what a dangerous woman she could be.

'I did nothing more than tap the man on the legs. It was his own lack of control that made him fall down.'

'That still amounts to an assault in the eyes of the law, madam,' Tennant said grimly. 'If I were you I would try and keep my deepest feelings under control in future.' He stood up. 'I shall expect you at Lewes Police Headquarters at eight o'clock tomorrow morning sharp.'

Meg rolled a fearful eye. 'But we live in Oakbridge. We shall have to get up at six.'

'Be sure to set your alarm,' said Tennant. 'Good evening to you.'

TWENTY-ONE

Jonquil eventually left the vicarage at ten, her tears, temporarily at least, dried up and a shadow of a smile on her face. Nick would in other circumstances have asked her to stay the night, regardless of the many Lakehurst eyebrows that would have shot up, but frankly he was afraid that William might get up to his tricks. During the evening Nick had gone to the upstairs lavatory and had received two loud knocks on the door.

'William, stop it,' he had ordered loudly, only to be rewarded with a third – but very gentle tap – before the ghost had retreated.

Nick had had the feeling that the loyal old entity was in a good mood because later that evening, after Jonquil had gone, Nick could hear the strangest shuffling on the landing. Going to the door of the living room he had listened carefully and had concluded that this blithest of spirits – to quote Noel Coward – was dancing Gathering Peascods or Big Breasted Susan or something of that ilk. He had thought then that the resident ghost somehow enhanced the house with its presence, a view not shared by Radetsky who arched his back and hissed at the noise. Nick had added his voice.

'Now, William, I want you to be quiet tonight because I feel in urgent need of sleep. Miss Charmwood has quite worn me out.'

He laughed at the double entendre but did not hear another sound until he was awoken by something pressing on his pillow. Slightly panicky, he switched on the light, but it was only the cat who had sneaked up in the night and crept on to the bed with him. Nick turned off the alarm and had another hour's sleep.

Ekaterina was having a horrible nightmare. She dreamed that her late husband had opened the door of her bedroom and was advancing slowly towards her bed. He looked terrible, his black skin peeling away from his bones and his baseball cap, worn sideways, pulled down over one decomposing ear. She tried to scream but as is the way with those in the grip of a bad dream no sound came out. Eventually she managed to make a noise and woke to find the bedroom empty but the door open, which gave her something of a shock. Getting out of bed she went down the silent, dark corridor until she came to the staircase. There was a child sitting on the stairs, she saw it quite distinctly before it faded into the shadows. Going down to the kitchen Ekaterina poured herself a brandy and sat there sipping until the first streaks of dawn shafted like anemones across the sky. Then she went upstairs and packed enough clothes for a few days' absence.

Her decision had been reached. In a few minutes' time she would get into her car and drive to London to put the house on the market with a top-flight estate agent. It was not that she did not like the place – she had loved it on first sight – but since Gerry's murder it had somehow become sinister. It needed a family in it to laugh and make a lot of noise. It was enclosing her and she would become immured if she did not make an escape. And since it was hers in her own right, paid for by her and with her own name on the deeds, she was free to sell it whenever she so wished. But where to go in the meantime? That was the puzzle.

Ekaterina suddenly sat down on her dressing table stool and cried her eyes out. Not for Gerry, though she had loved him once in an immature, girlish way. But because now something new had happened to her. For the first time she had got proper grown-up feelings for a man and – unbelievably – his daughters.

It was not the attraction of the castle. She could have purchased one of those without turning a hair, well a small curl anyway. No, it was Rufus Beaudegrave that she wanted, longed for him to take her in his arms and hold her tightly until the nightmare of Gerry's death and that poor girl who had been drowned in the moat was far behind her.

Ekaterina suddenly went cold all over. In the mirror, staring round the door and into the room, she could see the small child that had been sitting on the stairs. Terrified, Ekaterina looked straight into its eyes. The little boy smiled and waved his childish hand before vanishing from her sight. Scared nonetheless, Ekaterina grabbed her suitcase and ran down the stairs and into her car, then set off in the direction of London.

It was still early in the morning when Tennant knocked on Oswald's door. Today the inspector was wearing a lavender suit and purple tie as he had an evening appointment to appear on *Crimetime* – a regular monthly television programme that frightened yet fascinated the nation – and would have no time to change. So he was feeling fractionally overdressed as the front door opened to reveal a large man with a bald head and glasses who stared at him as if he had come from another planet.

'Good morning,' said Tennant pleasantly. 'I am Inspector Dominic Tennant from Sussex Police. I wonder if I could have a brief word with Oswald Souter please.'

'He's having his breakfast,' the bald man answered. 'But come in if you like.'

Tennant followed him through a narrow passageway to a room at the back where a television set was playing an early morning chat show. Oswald was gazing at it while shovelling in massive spoonfuls of muesli and spilling drops of milk on the plastic tablecloth. He looked up in some surprise as the inspector walked into the room.

'Oh hello,' he said offhandedly.

'Good morning, Oswald,' Tennant replied in ringing tones. 'Please carry on eating. I've only just popped in briefly.'

'What for?'

'For the reason that I am making enquiries into the death of Emma Simms, who, if you remember, was the girl found floating in the moat. Well, the post-mortem has revealed that she was knocked unconscious, then heaved into the water while still alive. That's a horrible way to go, don't you think?'

Oswald nodded, his mouth too full of cereal to utter anything.

'Shame,' he said monosyllabically, after swallowing.

'Did you know Miss Simms at all? Outside the Odds I mean?'

Oswald put down his spoon and regarded Tennant with a suspicious eye.

'No. I didn't even know the bear was her, if you see what I mean. I thought it was Jonquil. It wasn't until she squeaked at me that I realized. Then I sent her on her route.'

'Why? What was she doing?'

'Oh, just wandering around where she shouldn't have been.'

'Could you be more specific?'

Oswald attacked the last of his muesli. 'Not really,' he managed in between gulps. 'She was just ambling round the place and I had to tell her to get out of the way. Her big scene was coming.'

'You mean the Elizabethan Fair?'

'Yep. That was no time for her to try and see the rest of the show.'

'Was that what she was doing?'

'I guess so. She was just in the wrong place at the wrong time.'

The bald-headed man stuck his head round the door.

'Sorry, Inspector, but Oswald's got to run if he is going to catch his train.'

'All right, Dad, I'm going.' The young man stood up. 'Have you finished with me?'

'Yes, thank you. For the time being anyway.'

Oswald picked up a battered-looking backpack from the chair beside him and ran a protruding comb through his brownish hair.

'Well, see you later.'

'Goodbye.' And Tennant rose politely to his feet. The bald-headed man took a seat at the table and poured himself a mug of tea.

'Would you like a cup?'

'No, thanks very much. You're Oswald's father I take it.'

'Yes, that's right. It's just me and him. I lost his mother ten years ago.'

Tennant made the right noises, wishing that people would use another phrase when referring to death.

'I'm Norman, by the way.' The man stretched across the table and pumped Tennant's hand heartily. 'Pleased to meet you.'

'How do you do? It must have been quite a struggle for you bringing up the boy on your own.'

'It was. But fortunately Oswald has always had an interest in drama. I sent him to Kids Got Talent when he was only five and he wiped the floor with the rest of the bunch. Took the lead in everything. But lately he's been more concerned with the directing side. It was a boon to him when he joined the Odds. He's gone from strength to strength with them.'

'What did he make of Gerry Harlington?'

'Well, to be perfectly honest . . .' Norman leant across the table. 'Oswald didn't take to him one little bit. He came home and said "Dad, I don't reckon that fellow. I think he's going to muck the show right up." And wasn't he right? I went to the dress rehearsal and I saw that terrible dance Gerry did. It was diabolical.'

'Well, it seems everyone agreed on that point. And somebody murdered him as a result.'

'Yes, that was going too far, I must admit.'

Tennant didn't know whether to laugh or cry. He changed the direction of the conversation.

'Tell me about the stagehand who moved the dummy. Did you know him?'

'Charlie Higgs? Oh yes, I know him very well. The Higgses are a big farming family hereabouts.'

'And what about Charlie? Does he follow in the family tradition?'

'Yes. He went to college in Cirencester and learned all about agriculture properly. He's a true farmer. Yet he's always loved the stage but is too shy to take an active part. Great strapping lad, he is. He's the one who moved the body, you know. But then I expect that you *do* know.'

'We try to keep abreast of what is going on in the police force,' Tennant answered drily.

'Oh, of course you do. No offence,' said Oswald's father apologetically.

'I didn't interview him personally. But I intend to call on him now as a matter of fact.'

Mr Souter consulted his watch. 'I expect he'll be seeing to the milking at this hour. Do you know your way to Higgs Farm?'

'No, perhaps you'd be kind enough to direct me.'

And this the elder Souter did with much enthusiasm, even going so far as to draw little maps of the area illustrated with arrows and crosses.

Just as had been predicted, young Charlie, who stood six foot six inches high and had the orange hair and bright-blue eyes of a typical Sussex dweller, was fixing a massive herd of cows on to the milking machines. Inspector Tennant, mindful of his dandified clothing, had thrust his feet into a pair of wellington boots and made his way cautiously up the aisle to where Charlie Higgs stood amidst the swishing tails and mellifluous mooing.

'Good morning,' said Tennant cheerfully, and carefully produced his badge.

Charlie stared at it before replying. 'Oh, the big cheese, eh? I wondered if you'd come and see me.'

'Forgive me for leaving it so long. I think it was Constable . . .'

'Oh yes, a jolly pretty girl,' interrupted Charlie in an extremely well-educated voice. 'She had got quite the most attractive eyes.' His fair skin went rose pink. 'At least I thought so.'

'Yes, a very nice woman,' agreed Tennant.

'She told me her name was Morgana Driscoll. I enjoyed the whole interview.'

'I'll try not to ruin the illusion but I'm afraid I must ask you one or two questions.'

'Righto. Fire away.'

'Do you think we could go somewhere a bit quieter?'

'Of course. Mustn't spoil your lilac suit. I'll call Dave.'

Charlie proceeded to bellow the name several times until at last a wizened little gnome appeared from the far end of the shed and said, 'Yes, Charlie?'

'Take over, will you. I'm being interviewed by the police. An inspector no less.'

The gnome actually tipped his time-worn cap, a gesture so old-fashioned that Tennant felt momentarily as if he had stepped into a bygone age.

'How do, sir,' Dave said, and looked respectful.

Tennant felt touched and thought how manners maketh man and wished that the feral teenagers he had to deal with had been so instructed by their parents, who were probably just as bad anyway come to think of it.

'Thanks, Dave,' he said. 'Now, Charlie, where can we go where it's peaceful?'

'Come back to the farm and I'll give you a cup of coffee.'

With his opinion of the Higgs family rising, Tennant was not to be disappointed when he followed Charlie into their home. Mother was cheerfully feeding a basketful of small kittens with a bottle of milk and looked up and flashed a most attractive smile, while Dad was in the back office doing accounts. It turned out that there were four sons altogether and two of them had followed their father into the farming business.

'My eldest brother is an auctioneer. Works for Christie's,' said Charlie, with just a hint of pride.

'What a wonderful job. What about the rest of you?'

'Mike and I run the farm with Dad. Allen is an actor.'

'Really? Does show business run in the family?'

'Yes. Got it from Mum. She was a dancer with the Royal Ballet.'

'Well I'll be damned. I used to go to Covent Garden quite a lot – before the prices became horrendous. I expect I saw her.'

'You probably did. Now, Inspector, what was it you wanted to ask me?'

'A delicate question. I believe you moved the body out of the way on the night of the murder.'

'Yes. Yes I did. It was my job to take it to one side at the end of the show. And before you say anything let me tell you that it was as heavy as lead to shift. I thought that little tinker Oswald had stuffed it with stones or something. But it was extremely dark and I had to do it by what light was spilling from the acting area so I didn't get a chance to look at it.'

'I see. So you had no idea it was Gerry Harlington?'

Charlie looked slightly annoyed. 'If I had known it was his

body rather than a dummy I would have called the police immediately.'

'Of course you would. That was stupid of me.'

Tennant leant across the kitchen table at which they were sitting.

'Charlie, tell me. Can you think of anyone in the Odds who would like to have seen Gerry Harlington out of the way?'

The young man sipped his coffee thoughtfully, then said, 'Practically every one of them, I should imagine. But that doesn't mean that they did anything about it.'

'No,' Tennant answered slowly. 'It doesn't, does it?'

TWENTY-TWO

It was Araminta Beaudegrave who answered the telephone, speaking in her most grown-up voice. 'Fulke Castle. Can I help you?'

A woman spoke at the other end, saying rather breathlessly, 'Would it be possible to talk to Sir Rufus Beaudegrave please?'

Araminta paused, wondering if it was a member of the press corps who were still present – though admittedly in much reduced numbers – just beyond the gatehouse.

'Who would like to speak to him please?'

'It is Ekaterina Harlington here. Would you be one of his daughters?'

'Yes. Ekaterina it's me. Araminta. Oh, I do wish you would come and see us. We all miss you. Especially me.'

There was a definite sob, though stifled, from the person making the call.

'Oh darlings, I miss you too. How are every one of you?'

Araminta was fourteen and had mourned her mother more than the other girls. Now her jade eyes widened as a scheme presented itself loud and clear. She would lure the Russian woman into the net and persuade Daddy to marry her – not that it would take much persuading, she thought with a catlike smile.

'The girls are all right – and they all send their best love – but

Daddy is terribly miserable and nobody is sure why. He's not eating and he's not sleeping. He can hardly go about his daily duties,' she lied magnificently.

'Why is that?' asked the concerned Russian voice at the other end.

Araminta deepened her speech. 'Nobody knows. I realize you are always kind, dear Ekaterina, but I am begging you to be extra kind to him. He is so wretched.' She resumed her normal tones. 'He's in his study at the moment. I'll put you through.'

She jiggled a little black knob on the mini switchboard they kept in the hall and heard Rufus pick up, then she listened for a few moments to the ensuing conversation before quietly replacing her receiver.

'Rufus, is that you?'

'Yes.'

'It is I, Ekaterina.'

'My dear girl, where are you?'

'In London. I have put the house on the market. The estate agent will be driving down to see it tomorrow. I have given him the key.'

'But what about you? Won't you be there?'

'Rufus, I cannot go back to that place. It is full of bad memories. Besides, I saw a ghost. Truly I did. I am going to ask you a big favour.'

It was at this point that Araminta hung up, a contented smile on her face.

'And what might that be?' asked Rufus, his voice slightly perturbed.

'You remember once you asked me to come and visit with you. May I take you up on it?'

'Of course you can. Do, please. You can stay as long as you wish.'

'May I?' asked Ekaterina, suddenly out of breath again.

'You don't know how much I would like that.'

'Really?'

'Scout's honour,' Rufus replied – and there was a sudden electric silence.

*   *   *

Tennant had one more person to see before he called it a night
and went on to the television studios. This was Paul Silas, whose
secretary he had rung in order to make an appointment to call
on him. Judging Mr Silas as a pompous bastard Tennant had
done everything according to the book and thus was totally
prepared when he was ushered into a mahogany-furnished waiting
room with copies of *Country Life* and *The Collector* spread out
on the table before him. Picking up the former, the inspector
looked with envy at all the marvellous properties for sale. He
had always had a penchant for the moated manor house, but now
after all the terrible tragedy associated with the place he was not
so sure.

The secretary, who had dyed blonde hair and creepily long
scarlet fingernails, appeared in the doorway and gave Tennant an
appraising look. Unable to resist he fixed her with his ripe gooseberry glance and gave her a pleasant smile.

'Is Mr Silas ready for me?'

'Yes, Inspector, if you would like to go in.'

Ushering him into the inner sanctum with a great deal of fluting
laughter – though what about Tennant couldn't imagine – she
called out, 'The Inspector to see you, Mr Silas.'

'Thank you, Cheryl.' Paul stood up from behind his desk and
extended a hand. 'Inspector Tennant, to what do I owe this
pleasure?'

'Just a few routine questions, sir. Nothing to worry about
at all.'

Paul boomed a laugh and looked affable.

'I am not worried, Inspector. My conscience is clear and
therefore I have no need to worry. I suppose you have come to
ask about the wretched Emma Simms. Well let me tell you now
that a) I did not know her and b) I had no idea that Jonquil
Charmwood was fielding an understudy that night. Had I been
informed of such a thing – and I think as chairman of the Odds
I should have been –' pretentious old fool, thought Tennant – 'I
would have vetoed the whole idea. I run the Odds as a professional company, with professional standards, and a misdemeanour
like that would not have been countenanced in the real theatre.'

Tennant raised his eyebrows. 'Really?'

'Yes, indeed. I speak from experience. I appeared many times at the Old Vic and I can assure you that such a thing would never have been allowed. Of course, I knew Richard Burton extremely well. That is before he ruined his career by going to Hollywood.'

'Did you take major roles with him?' Tennant asked, looking wide eyed and innocent.

Silas regarded him with a certain amount of suspicion. 'No, I was a boy actor in several plays that called for young people. I would have gone on to the boards professionally but my father deemed otherwise.'

You and me both, thought Tennant.

'What did you think of Gerry Harlington?' he asked, changing the subject.

Paul Silas blew out his cheeks, looking momentarily like an ageing putto.

'Shyster,' he said. 'Complete charlatan. I believe he made one or two sub-standard films . . .'

'Actually those who have seen them thought they were quite good,' Tennant put in politely.

'That's as may be. But allow me to tell you that the man had no idea of ensemble playing. Nor anything else, come to that. I mean to say he attempted to ruin the whole show by inserting a hip-hop dance in the Elizabethan Fair. I ask you!'

'I believe there was quite a punch-up afterwards.'

Paul stared at his desk, a patronizing smile on his face.

'Boys will be boys. Somebody took a bit of a swing at him, I must admit.'

'And more than a swing it would seem. Tell me, Mr Silas, have you any idea who has done these murders? Because whoever it is has a warped and dangerous mind to say the least of it.'

Paul regarded his nails, not meeting Tennant's gaze.

'I have no idea, Inspector.'

'Did you know it was Meg Alexander who hit Robin Green on the back of the legs and caused him to fall down?'

The solicitor looked up sharply, his features undergoing a subtle change.

'Now you are speaking of the only true troublemakers that we have in the Odds. Mike Alexander would do almost anything to run the company and his wife is equally vicious. If you want to look anywhere for your murderers I think you need seek no further than that unpleasant pair.' He added hastily, 'This is in the strictest confidence, of course.'

'Of course.' The inspector was silent for a few moments before something naughty stirred within him and he asked, 'Have you played Lear?'

Paul Silas straightened his shoulders. 'Not yet but one day I intend to do so. I shall make it my swansong performance of course. Hopefully I shall go out like a flash of lightning.'

'I am quite sure your rendition will never be forgotten,' answered Tennant guilelessly.

It was the day of Gerry Harlington's funeral, the coroner having finally released the body. The church in Oakbridge was packed and Nick, who was conducting the service by special arrangement with the vicar of the parish and also to grant Ekaterina's heartfelt request, looked round at a welter of faces, some familiar but some unknown. He gathered from the sharp suits and predominance of tinted glasses that they were the Hollywood crowd. Then there were representatives of the family. Black men in full mourning gear with trilby hats that they swept off as they entered church; a very large lady in a purple dress and matching coat, tugging a little at her ample bosom, weeping discreetly into a small handkerchief; an ultra-chic woman with two round-eyed children, the boy dressed in a miniature man's suit, the little girl with bunches of curly dark hair. They must have flown in from America, thought Nick, and felt a deep regret that they had had to come to such a sorrowful occasion.

The Odds were out in force, Meg Alexander looking disgruntled having been charged at Lewes with assault, Mike wearing a respectful dark tie. Paul Silas was there with a plump woman who Nick presumed must be his wife. He had on his mourning face and one would think, looking at the old hypocrite, that a close relative of his had died. Estelle and Fizz were present, so was Annette Muffat wearing a huge pair of false eyelashes. Cynthia Wensby, she of the plain face, had made a great effort and slashed cyclamen lipstick in the region of her mouth, while Robin Green was, for once in his life, wearing a pair of very crumpled trousers. Barry Beardsley had torn himself away from the bunions and Jonquil Charmwood, getting back into her old and rather delightful ways, arrived breathlessly late. Sir Rufus Beaudegrave was in attendance and, sitting at the very back of the church, Nick noticed the two policemen, Tennant and Potter, quietly watching the congregation.

The vicar went to the doorway to greet the coffin and saw with immense sadness that Ekaterina, looking exquisite in a simple dark suit by Chanel, walked alone behind the casket, borne aloft by the undertakers. She took her seat beside her masseur, Ricardo, who today resembled, yet again, a modern version of Rudolph Valentino. The organ burst forth with the Shaker hymn, *Lord of the Dance* – a touch ironic Nick thought – and the congregation, usually vocally weedy and thin, were treated to the glorious sound of black people singing their hearts out. In a way, Nick thought, Gerry Harlington had had the last laugh on them all. He was going out in a blaze of glory.

After the cremation, which was very small and quiet with only Ekaterina, Nick and the lady in the purple dress – who turned out to be Gerry's mother – present, they went back to the moated manor where the firm of London caterers had started the wake. And what an occasion it was. Regardless of the fact that Gerry had met his end in such a brutal and terrible way, Nick saw the usual reaction of everyone present. Everybody heaved a mental sigh of relief that they were still alive and attacked the wine and canapés with gusto. Paul Silas, as usual, was holding forth.

'Of course we respected Gerry's modernistic approach, though we did not necessarily agree with it,' he was lying to a man who could have been a cousin of Danny DeVito, being small and rotund and dwarfed by a pair of enormous horn-rimmed glasses.

'Sure,' answered the other, 'I guess a lot of us felt like that. But I can tell you that Gerry was a peach to handle.'

'Oh, you have worked with him then.'

'You could say that. I'm Buddy Temple. I directed the Wasp Man pictures. And the cult movie *King of Bamboo*.'

The look on Silas's face was indescribable. Varying expressions rushed across it until they finally settled on an egregious grin.

'My dear sir,' he said, his voice suddenly melodious, 'how very nice to meet you. Of course, I have been associated with theatre for many a long year. I first worked with Richard Burton, you know.'

'Is that so? Well, I'll be damned. I was assistant to the assistant clapper boy on *Alexander the Great*. Boy could that Burton put away a drink. Tell me, are you acting now?'

Paul's voice and face both dropped dramatically. 'No, alas, my father took me away and made me study law. I am just a country solicitor.' He laughed heartily. 'But I am chairman of the Oakbridge Dramatists and Dramatic Society so I am still very much in touch with my first and only love.'

'Well, that's great. Keep it up. Oh, hi Nicole. I didn't know you were here.'

The woman who had joined them was very thin and had blonde hair, her face being almost completely hidden by an enormous pair of dark glasses. She had three heavily set men who walked one step behind her.

'I was in Gerry's first film when I was just starting out in Hollywood,' she answered in a husky and somehow terribly familiar voice. 'I felt I owed him my respects.' She nodded and smiled at the rest of the crowd who had suddenly gathered round and went on her way, her three heavies following.

'Crikey,' said Barry Beardsley, 'wasn't that Nicole . . .?'

'Keep your voice down. She's obviously here incognito. Just remain cool and calm.'

'Well you've gone the colour of a blood orange if I may say so.'

'No you may not,' Paul Silas answered furiously and moved off in the path that the Hollywood star was taking.

How Ekaterina stood it Nick never afterwards knew. She spoke to everyone, comforted Gerry's mother, his sister, his niece and nephew. Talked to the celebrities, to the Odds, and behaved with a quiet dignity throughout the whole proceedings. Eventually the entire company left, the Hollywood set to London and good hotels, Gerry's relations to The Great House in Lakehurst. The Odds, some flushed with wine, others with excitement, most with both, had wended their way to their various homes. The wake was over and there remained only the vicar, the widow, and Sir Rufus Beaudegrave. The caterers were busy clearing up and out of the way.

'Will you be all right here on your own?' Nick asked.

'I am actually staying at Fulke Castle with Sir Rufus and his family.'

It was then that another moment crystallized in the vicar's brain. It had just been a look, nothing more than a mere glance between them. But now it took on a greater significance. Nick felt quite certain that Sir Rufus loved the beautiful Russian and had plans for the future in that direction.

He was glad. He liked them both and realized that though it would shock convention, Nick personally approved of the match. Driving back through the gloaming, he felt uplifted and when he reached the top of the hill glanced round at the glorious surroundings and was grateful to be alive.

'All things bright and beautiful,' he sang, and a blackbird in a nearby tree carolled out a tuneful reply.

TWENTY-THREE

Nick parked his car in West Street and made his way briskly to The Great House. For some reason the street lighting had failed in the High Street and he had the delightful experience of seeing the houses lit from within, casting their illumination on what passed for the pavement. His thoughts went back to the eighteenth century when Lakehurst had hosted a powerful gang of inland smugglers, who had walked, a hundred strong, to Romney Marsh and there rustled sheep, whose fleeces had been shipped on to the wool merchants of Flanders. This had led to bigger things, brandy for the parson, baccy for the clerk, in the words of Rudyard Kipling. Nick wondered whether, had he been alive in those days, he would have traded with the smugglers, and thought with a grin that he probably would.

He was humming *A Smuggler's Song* as he turned into the entrance to the pub so that he didn't notice he was being followed by another figure who tapped him on the shoulder.

'Hello, Nick.'

He turned and saw Kasper. Before he could speak the doctor

said apologetically, 'I'm terribly sorry I couldn't make the funeral. I had an urgent call to a patient just as I was about to leave the house. Unfortunately I was on duty and had to go. How was it?'

'If you can ever say those occasions went well, then this one did. You will never guess who was there.'

'Who?'

'Nicole . . .'

But the rest of the vicar's words were drowned in a huge burst of laughter from inside the pub and the doctor had to lip read to understand the rest of the sentence.

'Really? Good God. So the late Mr Harlington must have been highly regarded.'

'She said she was in one of the Wasp Man films and that it gave her her first big break in Hollywood.'

Jack Boggis was standing at the bar, impatiently waving a five-pound note about. He turned on hearing someone approach him.

'Evening. The time you wait to be served in this dump is diabolical. Trouble is there're a lot of damned foreigners staying here.'

Nick glanced round and saw that there were several of Gerry's black relatives also waiting for service and that the barman and bosomy young woman helping him were run off their feet.

'Patience is a virtue, Jack.'

'Don't you start quoting things at me, Vicar. I'm dying of thirst here.'

Kasper put on his professional voice. 'How often do you get these symptoms, Mr Boggis?'

'They're not symptoms. You're just touting for business, Doctor.'

Kasper looked mournful. 'Alas, no. That is very far from the truth. The fact is that extreme thirst, regularly suffered, is a sign of type one diabetes. Tell me, do you frequently feel the need to urinate?'

Jack's several chins wobbled like that of a turkey cock. 'I don't think that that was a suitable question to ask in a public place.'

'I do hope you haven't taken offence at the mention of urin-ation, Mr Boggis. It is a perfectly natural function let me hasten to assure you.'

'I shall keep my functions to myself, thank you,' Jack answered, and turned away from them.

'Well, that's as well,' said the vicar in a whisper and he and Kasper once more giggled like a pair of naughty schoolboys.

It was at that moment that Inspector Tennant walked into The Great House and looked round him, then, seeing Nick and the doctor, made his way towards them.

'Good evening to both of you. I thought the funeral went as well as possible in the circumstances, Vicar.'

'Thank you. I did my best. Ekaterina Harlington is a brave and courageous woman.'

'And beautiful. I don't think she'll have to wait very long before suitors come knocking at her door.'

'How poetically put,' said Kasper. 'I like your turn of phrase, Inspector.'

'Thanks. Obviously she was my prime suspect at first but her – and Sir Rufus's – alibi were confirmed by one of his young daughters. Funnily enough, I was glad.'

'Why do you say that?' asked Kasper.

'Because one is supposed to remain utterly impartial at all times. Nonetheless, I liked the woman. You do realize who her father was, don't you?'

'No,' said Nick. 'But I'll bet it was some Russian oligarch.'

'It wasn't some Russian oligarch, it was *the* Russian oligarch. It was Grigori Makarichoff.'

Kasper exploded into his beer, which had finally arrived. 'Good heavens! She must be one of the richest women in the world.'

'I think,' answered Tennant slowly, 'that she probably is.'

'I believe that this must be one of the most beautiful places I have ever seen,' said Ekaterina quietly, looking at the castle and the moat taking on the colours of flowers as the sun sank behind the trees. She and Rufus smiled at one another, totally at peace for the first time that day; a day on which Gerry Harlington had finally been laid to rest unlike poor Emma Simms whose body was yet to be released.

'Despite it being the scene of your husband's murder?' he asked directly, wanting to sort the matter out, not wishing for her to have any feelings of horror about his ancestral home.

'Yes,' she said, 'even despite that. You see, I think this ancient place has seen its share of violent death in its time. If one were to grieve over everyone who died here then one would spend one's entire life grieving.'

'Yes, but Gerry . . .' He could not go on.

'You know that I had decided to divorce him,' Ekaterina answered. 'I loved him once, when I was young and ugly. But I realize now it was just childish infatuation.'

Rufus stood up and went to get the decanter. The firelight reflecting in his hair and on his aristocratic features.

'I don't believe that you were ever ugly,' he said, his back to her.

'I was hideous. I even had a squint.'

'Then the ugly duckling has become a swan.'

He turned round, put the decanter down and, taking her in his arms, gave her a kiss that rocked her to the soles of her feet.

'Sorry to pick such a bad day,' he said, stopping to breathe, 'but I just couldn't wait any longer.'

'I'm glad you didn't. I mean did. Oh hell, I don't know what I mean.'

'Then stop talking,' Rufus answered – and kissed her again.

Tennant had gone back with Kasper and Nick to the vicarage and there was drinking coffee as he had the drive to Lewes in front of him and tonight was minus the stalwart Potter.

'So what do you think?' he said to Nick.

'I think it's a damned good idea. Of course, you'll have to run it past Paul Silas.'

'No,' Tennant answered, 'as a matter of fact I won't. If I think that a reconstruction of the Son et Lumière will help the police with their enquiries then it must take place, as night follows day.'

'How will you organize it?' asked Kasper, genuinely interested.

'By telephone,' the inspector answered. 'I have an entire list of the cast and crew and I shall simply get my team to ring everyone and demand their presence in five nights' time.'

'Suppose somebody can't make it?'

'They will have to make it,' replied Tennant, 'or they will be charged for . . . I don't know . . . something or other.'

'Well, I shall certainly be there,' said Nick.

'Can I come?' asked Kasper.

'Yes, and you can bring with you anyone else who was in the audience that night. I want it to be as true a representation as we can make it.'

'What about Jonquil?'

'Like it or not she can play the part of Emma Simms.'

'She won't like it, I can tell you that.'

'Then she'll have to lump it.'

Nick cleared his throat. 'Have you got any suspects yet, Inspector?'

Tennant sighed and shook his head. 'It's a messy case, this one. There are so many people involved. It literally could be anyone. All I know is that somebody climbed the spiral behind Gerry Harlington and sent him flying forward to his death.'

'And you think that Meg Alexander's attack was a mere coincidence?'

'Yes and no. I can imagine him lurking in the shadowy doorway, probably wearing a cloak as disguise, and when he saw Robin Green fall backwards he seized the moment and rushed out and gave him a hearty push.'

'Whose duty was it to throw the dummy?'

'Adam Gillow, the man who got stuck on a train. He was to crouch down and heave it over at the same second.'

'Oh dearie me, what a chain of circumstance. If Adam hadn't have got himself stuck perhaps Gerry Harlington would be alive today.'

'Who knows?' Tennant answered.

'I rather think he signed his death warrant when he did that hip-hop dance in the Elizabethan Fair,' said Nick slowly.

'And I rather think you are right,' said Tennant quietly.

TWENTY-FOUR

Taking his seat in the now almost empty space that had housed the audience at the one and only performance of Son et Lumière, Kasper felt a thrill of anticipation creep down the length of his spine. Up in the window high above, the window that looked out from the Tudor banqueting hall, the doctor could vaguely see the outline of a man and woman, sitting close together, and four children of various sizes grouped round them. In the actual audience with him were old Alfred – who had announced loudly that he wouldn't miss it for the world, very much annoying Jack Boggis who had dismissed the reconstruction as piffle – and Madisson the beautician who was going into business with Ricardo. Looking round him Kasper could see that a dozen or so people were gathered to watch the re-enactment; the rest of the seats remained empty.

There were police everywhere. Standing at intervals round the side of the acting arena, in the changing tent, on the battlements, in every area backstage. And overall there hung a strange quiet that had almost a tangible feel to it. Anyone who spoke did so in a whisper and Madisson put it into words when she murmered to Kasper, 'Creepy, isn't it?'

The sudden blare of a loudhailer made everybody jump. It was almost obscene that such utter silence should have been broken.

'Ladies and gentlemen,' spoke the voice of Dominic Tennant, 'we are shortly going to run a reconstruction of the Son et Lumière which took place on the night of the murder of the late Gerry Harlington. I would like those of you in the audience to call out and raise your arm if you should see anything different – however small – that you witness tonight. Similarly backstage. This evening I am hoping that this visual evidence, showing us what actually occurred, will jog a memory that will lead us to unmasking his killer. Backstage, is everybody present?'

'Yes,' called a powerful hidden voice.

'Stagehands all there?'

'All here, sir.'

'Lighting men?'

'Here.'

'Right, let us begin.'

The lights were dimmed and the strange, evocative music that was on the beginning of the tape began to play. Rafael Devine's beautiful voice spoke the second stanza of the prologue into the incredible night.

'Fulke Castle, called by some the most beautiful castle in the world, stands alone on its small island, withstanding winter storms and summer sun alike. But in the year ten sixty-seven there was nothing where the castle now stands but a natural lake, its only inhabitants wild birds, when William the Conqueror granted a swathe of land in Sussex to his kinsman, Sir Fulke Beau de Grave who had fought at his side at the terrible and bloody Battle of Hastings.'

A spotlight was switched on and into it rode Paul Silas, somehow looking hunched and tired and not as bold and as brave a figure as Kasper remembered. He wondered whether to put his arm up but decided that this point was too minor to be of any interest.

The wonderful voice, playing with the words, caressing them as only a master of his craft could do, continued with the narrative. At this point Paul seemed to remember that he was giving a performance and sat up boldly, taking on the character which he was representing. The lights dimmed once more and the second scene came into view, Nick noticeable as a builder of Fulke Castle and Meg Alexander, looking thunderous, as the first Lady Beau de Grave.

It might have been eerie in the audience but backstage the atmosphere was worse by far. First of all a lot of petty arguments had blown up, mostly people picking on Jonquil Charmwood who tonight was playing the part of Emma Simms. She had been reluctant from the start but the caustic comments from various cast members, particularly Meg, had set her off into a crying fit. Potter had been called to intercede and had reminded the older woman that she was under charge for assault and any further trouble would be taken into consideration. Then

Robin Green had come face to face with her and let out a shrill cry of horror.

'You old cow,' he shrieked in a high-pitched voice and made as if to hit her.

A police constable had put his body between them.

'Now, now, Mr Green. You must learn a bit of self-control.'

'Self-control! The bloody woman nearly killed me.'

'Quiet, please. The second scene is beginning.'

Meg had joined Paul Silas, who had dismounted, and together they had walked into the acting area. She looked round her, then turned and stared off-stage. Kasper's arm shot up and he shouted, 'No.' The action came to a close and Tennant appeared looking odd in his modern suiting. He shaded his eyes with his hand and peered into the audience.

'Somebody called?'

Kasper stood up. 'Yes, it was me, Inspector. I don't remember Lady Beau de Grave staring into the wings like that during the original.'

'No, he's right, sir,' piped up old Alfred. 'She just kept looking at the builders.'

Tennant approached Meg. 'What are you looking at?'

'It's that beastly bear. She's wandering off towards the battlements.'

'Acting on instructions. You know damn well she went up there. You must have seen her when you attacked Mr Green. She must have hidden herself on the battlements.'

Meg looked like spite personified but said nothing.

'Very well. Continue,' said Tennant, and the action started again.

Scene three, the falling out of Sir Greville Beau de Grave with the See of Canterbury went through seamlessly from the audience's point of view, but backstage the actors were in turmoil. Charlie Higgs, whom Tennant both liked and trusted, had been briefed to keep an all-seeing eye on the movements of the stagehands while going through his own moves religiously. Thus he was standing by, ready to help the knights prepare for the big battle scene, the scene in which Gerry Harlington had lost his life.

First to climb up to the battlements went Jonquil Charmwood, feeling quite sick with fear. A second later Adam Gillow, who was taking the part originally planned for him, started to climb the staircase opposite, also leading to the battlements. The dummy was up there waiting for him, put in place by Oswald Souter before the show began. On seeing Adam start the ascent, so did Robin Green, both of them climbing quite slowly in their clanking armour.

Tennant motioned to Meg. 'Up you go, Mrs Alexander.'

'I must wait a second more. I mean, you want this show to be authentic.'

There was a shout from Charlie and his arm shot up.

'What is it?' asked Potter urgently.

'There's somebody missing.'

'Who?'

'I'm not sure – but there was a bloke in a cloak standing approximately where I am now.' He moved forward a few paces.

Tennant came up. 'What did you say?'

'Charlie says there was somebody standing where he is now but he doesn't know who it was.'

'Are you sure it was a man?'

Charlie looked Tennant straight in the eye. 'All I can say is that it looked exactly like a man to me.'

Up in the Tudor banqueting hall, Ekaterina cuddled closer to Rufus. 'Why have they stopped?'

'I'm not sure. Something must be going on backstage.'

They all stared down into the pit of darkness that was the audience arena. Then Perdita said, 'Look, there's someone moving down there.'

Everyone peered and could see a vague figure behind the police cordon, creeping so cautiously that it was quite possible it would escape detection. Rufus rose to his feet and banged as hard as he could on the Tudor window but this, by the very nature of its fabric, could not do with much ill-treatment and after a second's hesitation, he said, 'Ekaterina, look after the girls. I'm going down to catch the fellow.'

'Oh darling, be careful. He may be armed.'

But Rufus had already gone, clattering down the stairs, his feet ringing hollowly on the wooden flooring. Then a door opened and closed, and after that there was silence.

*   *   *

Tennant's eyes lost their sun-warmed fruit look and became as hard as green ice. He stared around him.

'Who was it?' he asked. 'Would you please come forward?'

Nobody moved or stirred and the atmosphere became riven with shards of suspense. A horse stamped an impatient hoof and a woman let out a little scream. Other than that there was an intense quiet.

'Well,' said Tennant – and his voice was full of menace.

'I don't think anybody is coming,' murmured Charlie, almost apologetically.

'No,' answered the inspector. 'It would appear not. Shall we continue.'

Like figures in a dream people released themselves from their trance and slowly made their way into their allotted places. The Son et Lumière started once more.

Rufus plunged into the darkness which lay beyond the brilliance of the arc lamps and suddenly found himself hardly able to see a thing. He stood completely still for a moment listening to all the sounds of the night. Down on the moat, water fowl were moving slowly, the ploshing of their webbed feet quiet but distinct. A fox passed close to him, disturbing the long grasses, making a tunnel of sound as it went about its nocturnal business. A bird in a tree overhead suddenly gave voice, its sweet song sighing on the night wind. And then came another sound, the sound of a human being making its way stealthily towards the bridge.

Rufus rose to his full height and shouted, 'Hey you, stay exactly where you are.'

His words had the absolute reverse effect as somebody stumbled towards him and gave him a hearty shove in the guts. Rufus doubled over, completely winded, and as he gasped for air he heard the feet retreating over the span and away into the open countryside beyond. The next sound he heard was that of a car starting up.

It took him a few minutes to recover and when he had finally got his breath back he limped towards the castle and straight into the arms of Mark Potter.

'You all right, sir? You look a bit done in.'

'I'm OK. But I saw somebody through the window of the Tudor banqueting hall; he was creeping away and though I tried to attract your attention you couldn't hear me. So I came down myself to try and stop him but he hit me in the guts and winded me. Sorry.'

'Nothing to apologize for, sir. Are you all right to get back to the house?'

'Yes, I'll manage. And by the way, you can call off the search. I heard him drive away by car.'

Potter let out a few expletives and then spoke into his phone. Almost immediately several police cars that had been parked just beyond the gatehouse took off into the darkness.

'Trouble is we don't know which direction he was going in,' he said.

'No,' said Sir Rufus, 'we can only hope you catch him.'

In the acting area Tennant's phone went and he made an announcement into a loaded atmosphere which had become almost overwhelming.

'Come on, let's get on with it.'

The horses, which had been growing restive, now charged at full belt at one another and in the audience Madisson said, 'That's Ricardo on the left. He looks good on a horse, doesn't he?'

'Very good. I understand you are going into business with him,' the doctor whispered back.

'Yes. My beauty salon is doing really well so I've decided to open up one of the rooms as a massage salon. He can do all the usual treatments, hot stones, hot oil and all.'

But her voice died away as the acting area was plunged into sudden darkness and a brilliant spotlight came up on two figures fighting on the battlements. Knowing that this was how a murder had been committed everyone in the audience fell totally silent, a feeling that was echoed backstage as well.

Robin had obviously been briefed to fall over at the exact moment when he had been hit by the stick. Consequently, he fell back and came face to face with Meg Alexander.

'You old bitch,' he said indistinctly, speaking through his helmet.

'You deserved it you arrogant bastard. You couldn't act your way out of a paper bag.'

'And who do you think you are?' he retorted. 'You and your

bloody husband tying to lord it over the rest of us. You're a pair of fucking little nobodies.'

'Oh!' she said, and began to make her way, clumping down the spiral.

Adam Gillow, not quite certain what to do, ducked down and simultaneously threw the dummy over. It came hurtling towards the ground and landed on its head. On the tape came the sound of a body hitting the earth and crunching as it did so. From the back of the audience Fizz let out a long and terrible scream and continued screaming at the top of her voice until Kasper got up from his chair and hurried to her side.

'My dear young lady,' he said, 'you really must get a grip on yourself. I know this is terrible for you – but it is for us all.'

She looked at him, her face twisted by the agony she was feeling. 'But that fall just now. It was so realistic. It reminded me vividly of the recent tragedy,' she lisped.

'But it was only a dummy,' he said, and his words ran in his ears like an echo, thinking of when he had eye-witnessed a brutal killing and but for those words would have gone to help.

They could hear the yelling backstage and Estelle said, 'Oh my God, that's Fizz. I must go to her.'

'You'll do no such thing,' said Tennant testily. 'I don't want any one of you to move.' He turned to Jonquil who had come down the spiral staircase last, following Meg Alexander and Robin Green. 'Now, I think at this stage Emma must have spoken to someone. Oswald, where are you?'

The youth sauntered up. 'You wanted me?'

'Yes, I do. You told me that you ordered Emma to get moving, that her big scene was coming. So that must have been around about now.'

'Yes. Yes, it was.' He approached Jonquil and said, 'What are you doing here? The Elizabethan Fair is on soon. Get back to the changing tent.' He turned to Tennant. 'I said something like that, anyway. Then I marked it down in my stage management book. See.' And he shoved the book under the inspector's nose. It was written in meticulous handwriting and had been done, quite extraordinarily, with a fountain pen which abruptly changed to the use of a biro halfway through.

Tennant looked at it and very slowly a light began to dawn

and there came that mercurial moment when the whole thing finally slipped into place.

'Why did you change pens directly after the murder?' he asked.

''Cos I lost my fountain pen. I was annoyed about that because my dad gave it to me for a prize I won.'

'Oh what a shame,' said the inspector, silken-tongued, and he slipped his hand into his breast pocket and produced a pen. 'Try this one for size.'

'Thanks. Why it looks just like mine. In fact, it *is* mine. There's that little scratch on the clip. Where did you find it?'

'You must have dropped it on the spiral stairs when you went up to murder Gerry Harlington,' Tennant said quietly.

Oswald stood frozen to the spot, then shouted out, 'You horrible old fucker. Go to hell,' and bolted as fast as an Olympic champion. Two constables tried to bring him down but nobody had the speed. He reached the moat and dived in, ready to cross to the other side. But it was Potter, who had joined the Police Sports Club and concentrated on tennis and swimming, who kicked off his shoes and brought him in, shivering and shaking, to where Tennant awaited him – like the angel of death.

TWENTY-FIVE

A dinner party was being given by Sir Rufus Beaudegrave to celebrate his new-found happiness, the coming of Christmas and the closing of the case. It was a black-tie occasion and Potter had been forced to go to Formal Tailor and hire evening dress, in which he felt somewhat uncomfortable but extremely grand when he saw himself in a full-length mirror. He had bought himself an evening shirt and was wearing a pair of cuff links left to him by his father. He had called in on his Welsh mother on the way to the party and she had said, 'Oh Mark, you do look fine. You really ought to get yourself a suit like that.' And Potter, hero of the hour because he had made an underwater arrest, rather thought he just might.

He and his boss, who was looking like a wicked pixie in his

formal dress with his great green eyes alight with some inner thoughts, were sharing a car and a driver so that they could have a drink and relax. And they both let out an appreciative cry of 'Look at that,' as the car crossed the bridge and they saw the castle in all its wondrous symmetry, fully lit up by floodlights.

'It has to be the most beautiful place in the world,' said Potter. 'Don't you think so, guv?'

This was a name he used for Tennant in moments of extreme emotion and Dominic, who didn't like the word much, just smiled to himself in the darkness.

Three months had passed since the Son et Lumière and the Yuletide was almost upon them. Sir Rufus had been out on the island and had brought in greenery and holly and ivy and had had Ekaterina and his four girls working on the decorations so that the castle was transformed into a thing of exquisite beauty. In the great entrance hall stood a massive tree which was decorated entirely in red and green tartan. And in the Tudor dining hall, which had been splendidly set up for the occasion, stood another large tree, this one the family one, with ancient decorations hanging on it, some of which probably dated back to Sir Rufus's childhood. To add the finishing touches to the Christmas sparkle there was a roaring log fire in the enormous grate and the sounds of a harpist playing gently, greeting the guests as they made their way in.

Ekaterina had never looked more beautiful, glowing from within, gracious and elegant in an emerald evening dress by Gucci, not a skinny thing like a nightdress but a romantic ball gown with lace sleeves and a full and swishing skirt. As for Sir Rufus, he seemed years younger, standing beside Ekaterina and saying 'Hello' to all who made their way up the ivy-bannistered stairs. His four girls were also on the receiving line, dressed in their party frocks, polite and charming as always. The two little ones, Perdita and Ondine, with whom they had had tea, made a special fuss of Tennant and Potter, Perdita giving Potter a kiss on the cheek which rather pleased him.

They were all present; all the people who had been involved in the tragic events, with one or two notable exceptions. The Alexanders had both received a stern warning; she for assaulting Robin Green; and he for running away from the police reconstruction of the Son et Lumière to attend an audition for *Royal Hunt of the Sun* at Lewes Little Theatre and attacking Sir Rufus into the bargain. The other absentee was, of course, Oswald Souter.

Tennant had felt rather sorry for him. Along with almost every other member of the Odds he had been driven mad by Gerry Harlington's lack of directing skills and the last straw for everyone had been the hip-hop dance in the middle of the Elizabethan Fair. But a very slightly crazy mind had been driven over the edge and Oswald had done what a dozen or so other people had thought about. But it was the murder of Emma Simms which had been both cruel and vicious. Still, Tennant had to admit that with a good defence barrister and a sympathetic jury the boy should get off with a relatively light sentence.

Yet all these thoughts were swept from his mind when he saw a surprise guest. Black headed, slim, dressed in red, his heart actually jumped in his chest as he looked in the direction of Olivia Beauchamp. Standing on either side of her were the Reverend Nick Lawrence, in a dinner jacket and a dog collar – a somewhat strange combination – and Dr Kasper Rudniski, dashing beyond belief. Tennant advanced on her.

'Hello, Olivia,' he said, and, taking her hand, kissed it in the old-fashioned way.

She gave him a look from those dark dreamy eyes of hers but what was in their depths he could not fathom.

'Hello, Dominic,' she said, and smiled.

Over in a corner, Paul Silas had taken on the role of Bluff King Hal and was looking about him at the roistering scene with a merry glance. Standing with his back to the fire, rocking back on his heels slightly, he was saying to anyone who would listen, 'By Jove, this is a very fine occasion, is it not? Very kind of Sir Rufus to host it. I wish one and all the compliments of the festive season.'

'Thank you, Mr Silas,' answered the Polish doctor. 'I return them to you.'

Further down the hall, dressed in rather garish colours but for all that having made an obvious effort, were Estelle and Fizz, holding forth about their time in the theatre. Nick, looking round him, thought what a good occasion this was and, staring at

Ekaterina and Rufus, hoped fervently that they would do the decent old-world thing and marry one another. He could rather imagine himself doing the blessing and smiled at the thought. But a butler was announcing in stentorian tones, 'Ladies and gentlemen, please be seated.'

There was a general scraping of chairs as each took their place where their allotted name cards indicated. As luck would have it Tennant found that Olivia had been placed next to him and felt determined that this stroke of good fortune would not pass him by.

'I am so glad to see you back safely,' he said. 'I've thought about you.'

She turned on him an amused glance. 'Did you get my postcard?'

'It's still on my mantelpiece.'

'Do you like your new flat?'

'I love it. Olivia, will you come and have dinner with me?'

'In your place? Or elsewhere?'

'I think elsewhere to begin with.'

'Yes,' she answered. 'That is a very pleasant idea.'

Paul Silas rose from his chair. 'Ladies and gentlemen. I crave a moment's silence.'

Pompous old fool, thought Nick, Kasper and Tennant simultaneously.

'I would like to propose the health of Sir Rufus Beaudegrave and to thank him for his congenial hospitality in inviting us all here tonight.'

'Hear, hear,' cried Robin Green who was attired in an evening suit that reeked of mothballs and had once belonged to Robin's father.

'It is marvellous for us humbler mortals to be invited within these magnificent portals . . .'

Oh dear, thought Potter, and his lips must have moved because Sir Rufus's eldest, Araminta, winked at him and he found himself getting a little flushed.

'. . . and I am sure that we can all get a sense of the place's fantastic history.'

He rambled on and everyone stopped listening politely. Jonquil, looking very pretty in pink, whispered to Nick, 'I owe you a dinner. Would you like to come?'

And he heard himself answering yes with a certain enthusiasm.

The toast finally ended. 'And I would call on you all to raise your glasses to Sir Rufus Beaudegrave.'

Everyone stood and Kasper called out, 'Coupled with the name of Fulke Castle.'

'Sir Rufus and Fulke Castle,' they said.

And outside, the frosty moonlight blended with the lights that shone on that ancient and venerable building, while the moat glistened silver in the darkness.